TRIAL OF FIRE

Metaha saw the two great beds of coals, the red heat glowing in the twilight, and watched as the warriors plunged the points of their lances into the fires. He stood still as his clothes were removed. Then he started forward through the line of warriors.

The ground burned his feet. Warriors held out their lances, burning his flesh. Topai held his lance against Metaha's thigh, and pain flooded his body. Waseta had no smile for his son. Instead the old chief held his lance against the side of Metaha, scorching the soft flesh black as night.

Metaha had never known such pain, but he did not call out. He held the pain inside himself, praying to the sky spirits that there would be strength to endure. . . .

SPIRIT WARRIOR

BY G. CLIFTON WISLER
A SPUR AWARD WINNING AUTHOR

ZEBRA BOOKS

KENSINGTON PUBLISHING CORP.

ZEBRA BOOKS

are published by

Kensington Publishing Corp.
475 Park Avenue South
New York, NY 10016

Second printing: March, 1989

Printed in the United States of America

The Brazos River gets its roots in the broken hills and barren mesas of the Llano Estacado, the great arid plain that covers most of what we know today as West Texas. From the Llano the river carves its way eastward through a hard land, creating an oasis of green amidst a sea of cactus and scrub mesquite trees.

Even today it is not a land of great cities, of giant industries. Only small towns with historic names like Graham and Palo Pinto have survived the years. The people use new methods, but farming and ranching are still their ways of life.

Change has come, though. The river no longer flows freely. Great dams control its waters, and roads crisscross its banks. The grip of man has come to harness the natural energy of the Brazos, and the river seems tame, defeated. It was not always so.

For those who walk the banks of the river and seek out the quiet places few have ever seen, traces of what was once there can be found. Old foundations of outposts of the frontier stage lines might be spotted. Arrowheads, carved from native flint, that have survived their makers can be uncovered in places that once echoed with the sounds of ponies and war cries.

And on certain evenings when the wind is still and the moon is bright, the great cliffs above the river seem transformed to the way they were a century and a half before. Shadows seem to dance across the waters, and strange cries echo across the land. It is the mourning voice of a people lost, a people erased by the hand of progress.

Not everyone hears the mournful hymn from the spirit cliffs. Not everyone sees the shadows dancing across the waters. Many rush by in the course of their

5

lives without caring to understand what has been there before. But to those whose hearts know the river and the lands beyond, whose ears know the sound of the owl and whose eyes see the hand of God in everything, these shadows of the past speak solemnly.

They tell of many things, of great hunts and savage battles. But of all stories, one is spoken with the most haunting of words. The words are like a whisper borne by the mourning winds. It is the story of a boy named Metaha and his trials of courage and wisdom. It is the story of a bond between a father and a son which not even death could break.

I

Long before the first white man ever came to the land of the great rivers, the red man was there. Long before the first thunder of a rifle echoed through the valleys of the bringer of life, the arrow flew into the hearts of deer and rabbit, and the buffalo ran to his death. Long before the sacred trees were cut down and shaped into the dwellings of the newcomers, those who had been there from the beginning, from the time the sky spirits first brought forth the sun and the moon, camped beside the great river in their hundreds.

Today they are gone, all of them. The buffalo no longer cloud the prairies with the dust from their hooves. The lodges of the great warriors, the songs of the children, the campfires where venison was smoked and stories were told—they have vanished like the sudden storms of summer.

Now the hand of the white man has shaped the valleys to his own liking. The waters that once surged across the land in their majestic freedom are broken by the will of man. The hills that were sacred to the

7

spirits of the sky feel footsteps of men who come without reverence or understanding.

Why do not the skies cry out in anger? Why do not the spirits shake the earth and cleanse the land? Why does not the hand of the most mighty reach down and sweep away that which has broken the spirit of the land?

Perhaps it is because the spirits know all. What is to be often comes without understanding; those who bring the challenge of change rarely wish to preserve what was before. This is why even the medicine cliffs yield to the sculptor of tomorrow. And as the life-threads of those who knew what was before are drawn to an end by the weavers of life, all is forgotten.

It should not be so. A man's heart should always hold a place for courage, for wisdom, should always respect what he could never conquer, even if he could erase. And it is for this reason that the spirits whisper the old stories from the shadows of the medicine cliffs. It is for this reason that the old voices speak, that the spirits still walk where the waters once gave life and accepted death.

Such stories should never be written. They were meant to be told by the light of a dying campfire under the clear and starlit skies of summer.

These stories were meant to be told by voices that had seen the spirits, that had been touched by the words of the old ones. But those who have seen and been touched grow old, and soon a great silence would take forever the old tales upon the same great journey that has already borne away the old ways.

Legends, myths, they are called. Tales made up in the minds of men grown too old for battle. To those who have never been touched by the words of the spirits, who have never watched the shadows walk sadly across the waters below the medicine cliffs, it must surely seem so. But who is to say what has been? Who is to say what is possible?

There was a time before the white man. Once the buffalo blackened the prairies with their numbers. And once there was a people whose courage and wisdom were honored by all. These people were called the cliff warriors by the Comanche and Wichita. Their brothers, the Caddo, knew them as the river people. But among their own people they were known as the Honey Dancers after a ritual dance they performed in the summer when honey was gathered from nearby hives.

They were a proud people. The sky spirits spoke to their chiefs, and none were braver in battle or more generous in time of peace. They walked the land with gentle steps, and they cared for all life they found. Even the smallest bird was sacred for its gift of song, and no man or beast was killed without reason.

The sky spirits loved the Honey Dancers. In the time before the sun and the moon, the sky spirits had reached down to the earth and carved out a great valley. Into this valley they poured the giver of all life, the great river. The river flowed from the spirit hills into which the sun died each evening, and it smiled upon the people with its bounty.

The sky spirits next set into the heavens the sun to warm the days and make things grow. The spirits also gave the people a moon to light the way for their warriors through times of darkness. One of the spirits took into his hand the dust of life and sprinkled it across the heavens, creating the stars. And then the greatest of the sky spirits reached into the river and made the first of the Honey Dancers.

Man, woman, child—they were all born from the river. And so it was that the river was their home. They took care to keep it pure and free, and even when the rains did not come and it grew small, they danced for its pleasure and sang to its greatness.

The Honey Dancers were a proud tribe with a rich heritage. They made the valley around them green and bountiful, and their numbers were like the grasses that grow beside the river. Their chiefs were recognized as among the wisest of all, and the courage of their warriors was never questioned.

One of the reasons the tribe was strong was a great test of manhood which all young men had to pass before joining the tribe as warriors. When a boy came to the time of young manhood, his father would present him to the tribe. Then the great trial would begin.

There were four tests to be completed. The first was the trial of the lance and war ax. The young man would stand a hundred feet from the ceremonial tree and hurl his lance. It had to penetrate the bark of the tree and hold fast. Next he would take the war ax and drive it into the heart of the tree below the lance. Having completed the first of his trials, the young man had demonstrated his skill with weapons.

The second trial was the test of fire. The young man would be forced to walk with bare feet between two beds of blazing coals. Warriors would hold red-hot spears close to his flesh. He had to endure all without crying out, even though he might be badly burned.

The test of fire proved a young man's loyalty and endurance. A warrior might be captured and tortured by his enemies, and those of his tribe had the need to know who would remain true to his brothers in spite of terrible pain.

The third test was the ordeal of manhood. It proved that a young man could stand alone and survive in the wilderness. Each youth would be stripped naked, and his hair would be shaved. White dye would be poured over his body, and he would be made to stand before the bright sun until the dye was baked into his flesh. He would then be taken across the great river, given but a knife, and sent out into the wilderness. If he returned before the dye was gone or was seen by a member of the tribe while the dye still showed, he would be killed instantly.

Many young men died in such a manner or fell victim to the elements or were killed by a hostile tribe or creature of the night.

There was also a fourth test, a trial of the spirit. It was spoken of only in the lodges of the priests and was sacred to each warrior in a manner known only to himself. Each test involved a journey. While on the quest, each youth was also ordained to bring back to his people a gift.

It was in this time that there lived among the Honey Dancers a great chief. His name was Waseta, which meant "of the great rivers." Such was his skill in battle that the neighboring tribes had been at peace with the Honey Dancers for twenty summers, for no tribe sought to bring down the anger of Waseta upon them.

Few white men came to the land of the Honey

Dancers, for those who ventured near were never heard of again. Many times the birds of prey circled above their wagons to mark the foolishness of a white man who had come to the lands of the Honey Dancers.

Such was the great wisdom of Waseta that tribes would ride five suns to seek his help in settling a dispute or stilling a quarrel. As his fame spread, the Honey Dancers grew wealthy from the presents brought to their chief.

But as great as Waseta was, his life was made hollow by a great sadness. He had no son. Four daughters had been born to him by Tahoa, his wife, but no sons. Many times Waseta had climbed the spirit cliffs to pray to the spirits of the sky, but the prayers were not answered.

In that time it was the custom for a chief who had no son to take the son of another warrior and raise him as his own. This was the way a new chief was chosen. But in his wisdom Waseta saw the great love each of the men of his tribe had for their sons, and he could not bring himself to cast out his own emptiness by heaping it upon another.

As the summers passed, though, the tribe worried over who would be the next chief. Waseta had grown old. Boltah, the chief priest, hoped his son would be chosen. Because of his rank in the tribe, it seemed a likely thing.

Waseta was in his fiftieth summer when he went at last to his wife, Tahoa. He remembered how they had run together through the fires of their fathers as children. He remembered summer skies they'd shared beside the river. He remembered the births of their daughters. His mind brought back to him the softness of her touch, the truth that came from her heart.

"Waseta, my husband," Tahoa said to him that night. "You must cast me from your lodge. You must take to your heart a younger woman, one who will bear you many sons."

Waseta looked into the sadness of her eyes and frowned.

"This I will not do," he said. "We have hunted the deer together many summers. We have shared the victories over the iron-headed white men, and you have tended to my wounds. I have eaten at your side, and you have brought my daughters into the world of light. We will lie together in the medicine places of my fathers one day even as we share this lodge."

But the people grumbled. Waseta knew that many tribes had been torn apart in wars to see who would become chief, and he did not wish such a curse to fall upon his people. Once again he journeyed to the spirit cliffs. There he stood alone by the great fires and prayed to the sky spirits. He ate nothing for seven suns. He tore strips of his flesh so that the blood would please the spirits. The haunting melody of his chant flooded the valley, but no vision came to him. When he returned to his village, nothing had changed.

Then one day a warrior rode into the camp of the Honey Dancers with grave news. White men were making a lodge from the sacred trees along the river beyond the sunrise. Waseta never delighted in the death of anyone, but he knew his duty. If one settlement was allowed, a second and a third would spring into being. From the Caddos Waseta had heard tales

13

of the white man's village beyond where the sun rose, and he feared this as he did nothing else.

The warriors put on their bright yellow paint and prepared for battle. They took out their war lances and chanted their prayers. Then they rode out to the place of the white men.

Waseta planned his battle carefully as always. He split his warriors so that they would come from three directions. As the sun began to sink into the hills, Waseta screamed out a war cry, and the Honey Dancers swept across the plains.

The air was filled with the flight of arrows, and war lances struck down the men and women of the settlement. Not even the children were spared, and soon the screams of women and the moans of men grew silent.

As Waseta walked among the dead, he heard a strange sound. It was the muffled cry of a baby. The chief walked to the log lodge and looked at the body of a young woman. Pushing her aside, he beheld a small baby boy, shielded from the arrows by the body of his mother.

The child was very small, and Waseta felt a sadness inside himself. He held the boy up to the warriors, and one of them prepared an arrow. Then a stillness filled the air, and a great eagle appeared in the heavens. The great bird circled the field of battle three times, then vanished into the clouds.

In the lore of the tribe the eagle was the messenger of the sky spirits. Waseta remembered his prayers, his lonely nights on the spirit cliffs.

"It is a great sign, my brothers," Waseta cried out. "This child is a gift from the sky spirits. He is to be the son so long denied me."

14

The warriors whooped and cried out. Their smiles were like a thousand suns. Then Boltah took out his lance and cast it into the earth beside Waseta.

"I am chief priest of this tribe," Boltah spoke. "You know nothing of these things. This is no sign. The eagle was sent by the sky spirits as a sign of our victory. All the whites must die! All!"

Waseta looked into the face of Boltah, then glanced at the child. Anger was all he could see in Boltah's face, anger and hatred. A white man had killed Boltah's father.

Waseta then looked into the shining face of the child. There was no anger in the small face. The child knew nothing of what had happened. Waseta remembered the hollowness inside him that was forever reaching out for a son, a son to share the buffalo hunt with, a son to pass on his wisdom to. The love the old chief felt was far stronger than the hatred in Boltah's eyes, and Waseta took up Boltah's lance and laughed.

"The sky spirits have spoken to me many times, Boltah," Waseta said. "They have led us to great victories, great riches. They speak to me again this moment. They say to me this child must not die!"

Waseta broke the lance and threw it on the ground. The old chief then mounted his horse and led the warriors home.

Many prayers were said that night in the camp of the Honey Dancers; many members of the tribe chanted for the long life of the child. Waseta bore the boy to the spirit cliffs and laid him naked before the spirits of the sky.

"Sky spirits, this is the sign you have sent me," Waseta said. "He holds the color of the sky in his eyes, and his hair is bright like the sun. Let him bring greatness to our people."

When Waseta returned to the village, he drew together the council of the warriors.

"This child will be called Metaha," Waseta said. "This means 'light from heaven.' He will be a brave and wise warrior."

The people rejoiced, and Waseta's heart was filled with gladness. Tahoa took the boy as her own, and the lodge was warm as never before.

II

The summers that followed blessed the Honey Dancers. At no time in the history of the tribe had so many deer run through the thickets, had so many buffalo been brought back from the hunt. As for Waseta, the chief walked the land with a new fire in his eyes. His life was full of laughter.

The boy Metaha was like a flash of lightning across a black sky. Never had there been a boy with brighter eyes, with keener ears. His smile was like the sun. Even in the days when he was too young to ride she walked among the horses, growing to know their ways. Old women whispered about the way he seemed to speak to the animals.

"It is as the story of Katai," one of them said. "The great chief spoke to the horses as a boy. In the battle against the first of the iron-heads, his horse heard his call and galloped across the field of battle to rescue him."

"And look into his eyes," another said. "Do you not see the sky, his father, in those eyes?"

"And his hair shines like the sun," said a third.

"Truly, we are blessed by the sky spirits."

But not all the Honey Dancers felt that way. When Metaha was in his sixth summer with the tribe, his old enemy Boltah led him into grave danger.

"Metaha, little son of our great chief," Boltah said to the boy. "Come with me and watch as I seek out our enemy, the rattlesnake."

Metaha had been taught by his mother, Tahoa, never to walk where rattlesnakes lived. He had been warned of the rocky places beside the river where the snakes abounded. But Boltah was a great man in the tribe, and boys did not walk away from a man who knew the ways of the medicine pipe. Such a boy might awaken to find himself ill with fever or even turned into a river frog.

So it was that Metaha followed Boltah, listening to the words of the priest with great care.

"In order to be a chief of the Honey Dancers, a man must have no fear," Boltah said. "You have never seen fear cross the face of your father. It is a lesson learned early. Come, little son of the sky, walk with me into the rocks."

Metaha was fearful, but Boltah was with him, and what happened to the boy would surely happen to the man. Metaha followed.

As they walked through the rocks, Boltah chanted softly. The rattling of the snakes seemed distant. Boltah beat his thigh with a stick, producing a sound not unlike that of a woodpecker.

Metaha listened to the sound, ignoring his mother's warnings about the snakes. The boy's eyes caught sight of the slithery bodies of many snakes, but his ears heard only Boltah's chanting. Suddenly the

18

chant died, and Metaha turned around. Boltah had vanished, leaving Metaha in the middle of the snakes' lair.

"Boltah?" Metaha called out to the priest.

The only answer was a hideous laugh.

"A snake should prove no great enemy to a son of the sky spirits," the priest said, laughing. "You should have no great trouble finding your way back to our village."

Boltah laughed again, then vanished into the brush.

Metaha stood alone in the rocks for a long time. He prayed that his father would come and take him home; he longed for the gentle voice and touch of his mother. He could hear the snakes all around him, and he shook with fear. Then he remembered what his mother had said to him about snakes.

"Remember, little one, the snake does not strike in anger," she had told him. "He only strikes at movement. Be still, and he will go away."

Metaha remembered Tahoa's words and froze. As he watched the snakes move through the rugged landscape, he remembered something else, something his father had taught him long ago.

"All creatures are sacred to the sky spirits, my son," Waseta had told him. "To harm without reason is to anger the spirits. Give over your soul to the spirits, my son, and you will fear no man or beast. Speak softly always to the creatures of the earth, and they will hear and understand."

Metaha remembered how he spoke to the horses, how they seemed to understand his words. He remembered the birds he'd spoken to, the wolf he'd met on a summer night beside the river.

"Snakes," the boy said, stepping forward softly. "I am Metaha, son of Waseta, chief of the people given to this land by the sky spirits in the beginning of the world. I bear you no ill, and I will not harm you. Let me go in peace."

The snakes stirred, and the sound of their rattles broke the stillness. They moved toward Metaha, and the boy took a deep breath. Then he stepped out among them, singing softly a chant his father had taught him.

> Spirits of the sky, hold me in your hands;
> Guard me from my enemies;
> Send me home to my lodge,
> To the warmth of my fire.

As he chanted, Metaha moved forward. The snakes seemed to sense the boy's words, and they moved away. Metaha walked on through the rocks, into the brush and back to camp. When he emerged from the trees at the edge of the village, Metaha had a smile on his face. He was met, though, by the stern look of his father.

"Where have you been, little one?" Waseta asked.

"I have been into the rocks where the snakes live," Metaha said quietly.

"You have been told by your mother the ways of snakes. Why do you go there?" his father asked.

"I was taken there by Boltah, Father," Metaha said.

His father stared into the youthful face of Metaha, then led the boy away into a grove of willow trees beside the river where the council met.

"My son, why did Boltah take you to the rocks?" Waseta asked.

"He told me that to be chief of our people, I must have no fear," Metaha said. "He carries many medicine pouches. I was more afraid of him than the snakes."

"My son, courage is a great thing," Waseta said. "It is a thing all chiefs must have. But to use courage in a personal test is not to use one's wisdom. What was gained by going into the rocks? Did you feel brave?"

"No, Father," the boy said.

"Did you prove yourself to the warriors?"

"No, Father," Metaha said.

"There are three things you must learn from what you have done this day," Waseta said. "One is that a man must never prove his courage to another man. If he has such courage, it will show itself on the day the spirits choose."

"Yes, Father," Metaha said. "But how do we know when the spirits call for it that we will be brave?"

"You will know," Waseta said. "Now the other things. To tempt the snake is not wise. I have seen the way you walk among the horses. You have the soul of the spirits, my son. Even the creatures of the night know you. But a man who has no respect for the snake, the wolf, and the panther is a man who offends the spirits. Such a man needs no enemy. He falls prey to his own pride."

"And the third thing, Father?" Metaha asked.

"You are young, my son," Waseta said. "But the son of a chief must know his people. Not all our people are like the old women who spin tales of the golden-haired son of the sky spirits. There are those who will hate you for the paleness of your skin."

"That is not my doing, Father," Metaha said. "Have you not told me that it is the heart that matters?"

"This is true, my son," Waseta said. "But it is also true that your skin, even in the heat of summer, will be more the color of the snow than that of your mother and father. For this there are those who will hate you."

"Boltah?"

"Boltah's father was a great warrior. In his prime, Boltah's father was killed by one of the white man's thunder sticks. This was in the time of the blue-jackets. They came after the iron-heads. There will always be others to come, others to kill."

Metaha seemed sad, and his father noticed.

"Are you sad, my son, because you find it hard to kill those who might be of your blood? You must know that your own mother and father were killed by our people."

"My father is Waseta, great chief of the Honey Dancers," Metaha said with fire in his eyes. "My mother is Tahoa, whose name means bright star. My place is beside you, Father, and I will ride with you against all our enemies."

"And the sadness?"

"Have you not taught me that to kill anything is to bring sadness?" the boy asked. "Even when I step on a crawling creature in the night I pray for it. Can killing a man bring less sorrow to me, Father?"

"It is always wise to have sorrow close to your heart, my son," Waseta said, taking the boy's hand and holding it against his heart. "Feel the beat of my heart, Metaha. For many summers this heart was empty. Only when I took you in my arms and held you up to the sky did I come alive."

"I will prove myself both brave and wise, Father," Metaha said. "If I fail, I will die."

"You must be only what the spirits command you to be," the chief said to his son. "Whatever you become will please your father."

When the great council met that evening, Boltah rose to speak. The priest bore a great frown on his face.

"I speak to this council of a matter of grave importance," Boltah said. "Waseta is a great chief, the greatest to lead our people since the time of Katai. But he grows old and has no son. A new chief should be chosen."

Waseta's face filled with anger, and the warriors of the council grew unsettled. Then Waseta rose.

"Boltah, you have made much medicine for our people," Waseta said. "You have spoken many words in this council. But it is not your place to choose the chief of our people. I have a son. He is not born of my wife, but he is the son of my heart."

"He is white!" screamed Boltah.

"He is a boy," Waseta said. "He came to us in the nakedness of youth. He knows only what we have taught him. His heart is as mine. Already he walks with the feet of Katai. His spirit is filled by wisdom and courage."

"It takes more courage to be chief than to walk among the snakes of the river," Boltah said, sneering.

"When the time comes, courage will grow in him

23

like the trunk of a tall tree," Waseta said. "He shows already more honor than some."

Waseta pointed his remark at Boltah as he would have pointed a war lance.

"The spirits cry out in the night for the life of this boy!" Boltah said. "I have heard their voices in my dreams."

"Your dreams lie to you, priest," Waseta said. "All who see this boy know how the spirits have marked him."

"You are fooled by hair of straw," Boltah said.

"You are deceived by a heart that can only hate, Boltah," Waseta said. "If you would open your heart to him, you would find he would run through your fire beside your own sons."

"The sky spirits will never allow a white boy to ride at the head of our warriors," Boltah declared. "We will all be cursed."

The warriors mumbled to each other, and Waseta strode out before the priest.

"Cursed?" Waseta cried out. "Have we ever known a time of more plenty? Have we ever known a summer when more children were given to the world of light? Were there ever more buffalo hides brought back from the hunt? Was there ever a time when our bellies were fuller? No curse comes upon our people."

The other warriors shouted their agreement, and Boltah turned away. The priest walked out of the council, and his medicine was never strong from that day on.

As the fires died in the darkness of evening, Waseta lay beside his son in the great lodge made from the skins of the many deer the old chief had killed. The boy lay quietly, feeling the warmth of his father's shoulder beside his own.

"Metaha, my son," Waseta said.

"Yes, Father," the boy said.

"Beware of Boltah," the chief said. "Never again find yourself alone with him. His heart is black with hatred, and he would find it easy to take your life."

"Should I fear him, Father?" Metaha asked.

"Fear is never the way of a chief," Waseta said. "Fear blinds a man from thinking. Know there is danger in the man. Know he means you no good. Always consider what he says to you before doing it. Never go with him anywhere."

"Is it not possible to speak to him as I did to the snakes, Father?" Metaha asked.

"It is always possible to speak with the spirit, little one, but Boltah's spirit is stained," Waseta said. "Such a blackened spirit will not hear your soft words. It is like the wolf who bears the scars of arrows. He no longer hunts for food. He seeks to call death in the night.

"Such a wolf is to be fought with great care, Metaha, for to him death is as nothing. It is always the creature or the man who has died inside that is the greatest enemy."

"Yes, Father," Metaha said.

"Now seek the peace darkness brings, my son," Waseta said, stroking the boy's soft hair. "Walk softly this earth."

The boy rolled over against his mother on the soft buffalo hide, and Waseta looked through the entrance of the lodge at the bright stars overhead.

"Spirits of the sky, guard my son," the chief said.

"He has the light of the stars in his eyes, and his laughter is like the morning sun. It warms the soul of an old man who has seen too many empty summers. Hold him close to your heart, spirits, as you have always held mine."

Then only silence filled the earth.

III

From the first Metaha was different. It was not only the sparkling blue of his eyes and the golden glow of his hair. It wasn't even his fair skin, for in the first moon of summer it turned bronze like the mountains.

The old women saw it first. They believed it came from the giver of all things, the greatest of the sky spirits. The touch of the stars, they called it. It marked the boy for future greatness. And as he grew, others came to believe it.

Metaha learned early the ways of the Honey Dancers. He did the dance of the hives and climbed to the spirit cliffs with his father to pray for the rains. From Tahoa he learned to work the skins of the deer and the hides of the buffalo. He made his own moccasins. He made the beadwork for his shirts.

From his father he learned the history of his people. A thousand times he listened to the stories of the great chief, Katai, who had first battled the iron-heads in the time of long ago. Katai was the favorite hero of the other boys, but Metaha preferred the stories of Waseta and his battles against the Comanches and blue-shirts from the lands below the river.

One morning in the moon before the buffalo returned to the grasses beyond the hills of Katai, Metaha was working at making new arrows. He had never hunted anything other than rabbits and squirrels, but many times his father had told him the value of strong arrows.

Metaha bound the sharp flint point to his arrow with great care. His hands were small, but the boy was strong and the point was soon in place. Then Metaha held the arrow up in the sunlight to see if the balance was true. An arrow that was shot from a strong bow by a steady hand would still miss its target if the balance was wrong. This arrow seemed perfect.

Metaha then took his paint out and made his marks on the side of the arrow. All of a warrior's arrows were marked in their own way, and Metaha was proud of the small sky sign he made on his arrows. No other boy had so beautiful a mark for his arrows.

"Is it a good arrow, my son?" Waseta asked as Metaha marked the arrow.

"It bears my mark, Father," Metaha said. "It is a good arrow."

"You will walk with me this night to the spirit cliffs to pray over them, my son," Waseta said. "The spirits will touch them with their eyes and cause them to fly into the hearts of your enemies."

"They are only arrows for killing rabbits, Father," Metaha said. "Rabbits are not enemies."

"A warrior's arrows are always at his side, my son," Waseta said. "An arrow may be used to kill a rabbit, but it is there to fight an enemy, whether man or beast. An arrow well made can save a warrior's life, can protect his people."

"Yes, Father," Metaha said.

That night as they stood together on the spirit cliff, the sky erupted with thunder. Bright flashes of lightning lit the sky, and the earth trembled. Waseta stood tall against the painted sky and held out his hands to the skies. In a voice that showed no trace of fear the chief screamed out across the emptiness to the sky spirits.

As if the spirits heard, the sky quieted. The earth shook no longer, and Waseta sat down alone on the edge of the cliff and closed his eyes. Metaha had watched his father sit in this fashion many times, and the boy knew it was not something that could be shared. He stood aside from his father and waited for the old chief to speak.

Time had no place on the spirit cliffs, and Metaha watched the stars cross half the sky before his father finished meditating. Then the man stood up and chanted quietly. Metaha listened, but the chant was one the boy had never heard before. Many of the words were unknown to him.

Metaha had heard his father speak of the very old words, the words spoken by the first of their people in the times of long ago. That was before the horse had first been given to the Honey Dancers by the sky spirits. Before that night Metaha had never heard the old chants, the medicine prayers to the old ones. When Waseta finished the chant, he turned to the boy.

"Bring your arrows, my son, that the spirits of the sky might touch them with their eyes."

Metaha gripped his arrows in his small hand and carried them to where his father stood. Waseta led the boy to the very edge of the cliff and spread his legs apart so that Metaha grew nervous. The wind blew the boy's breechclout against his thighs, and the hair was swept away from his face.

"Speak now to the spirits, my son," Waseta said, stepping back from the boy.

Metaha trembled. He was fearful that he might fall into the river far below. He calmed himself, though, and looked out beyond the valley at the heavens.

"Spirits of the sky, look down with your eyes at what I hold in my hands," Metaha spoke. "Speed my arrows to their targets."

Metaha stepped back from the edge of the cliff, but the hand of his father stopped him.

"You have not spoken to the spirit of yourself, my son," Waseta said. "Pray to the sky for what you would have sent to you."

"Spirits of the sky," Metaha said, feeling very small in the midst of the wide and violent sky. "I am Metaha, son of Waseta, great chief of the Honey Dancers. I am the one you sent to my father to walk beside him through the summers of his old age. Spirits of the sky, make me worthy of my name and my father. This is all I ask. It is enough for any man."

A terrible flash of lightning blasted over the hills across the river, and Metaha trembled. He wanted to run away from the cliff, but he could feel his father's eyes on his back. He would rather die in the waters below the spirit cliff than show fear in front of Waseta.

As the boy stood still, the wind blew stronger, tearing his shirt open so that his bare chest was exposed to the sky. Thunder boomed out all around him, but the fear left him. In its place was a sudden feeling of belonging. His feet grew solid, and it was as if he had been on the cliff always.

As his chest filled with pride and the fear left his face, the wind stilled. The clouds were swept away, and the stars sparkled overhead. The moon danced above the hills and showered the cliff with light.

"The spirits of the sky are pleased with you, my son," Waseta said, putting his great hand on the boy's shoulder.

"Father, I was afraid," Metaha said, collapsing against the firmness of his father's side.

"Metaha, little son of the sky," Waseta said, "when I first was brought here by my father, I had been already to the buffalo hunt. I had killed many deer. But when the winds raced across my face, I shook with the terror of the night.

"It is the way of the spirits to cause fear in one who comes to them for the first time. But fear, my son, is only confusion. This I have said to you before. The spirits saw the nature of your heart, my son. They know you now and forever more. They know you walk in the way of your fathers, that you will bring honor to them. This is no small thing."

Metaha smiled at the words of his father, and the man led the boy to the medicine circle and sat down beside him. There was a great frown upon the man's face, and Metaha could tell that his father was troubled.

"You are troubled, Father," the boy said.

"It is not an easy thing to be chief of our people, my son," Waseta said. "The warriors will soon ride out to hunt the buffalo. The food from this hunt will keep our bellies full when the cold winds come."

"I know this, Father," Metaha said.

"I have ridden out to hunt the buffalo since the

time when I first passed the trials of manhood. All these summers I have ridden the plains alone, knowing only the lonely song of the warrior. I have not felt your mother's hand nor known the soft laughter of a child.

"I am in the autumn of my journey through the world of the flesh, my son. My bones grow cold in the night, and my teeth are yellow with age. My bow arm is still strong, but I do not ride with the wind as I did in my youth. I would stay here in the land I love, in the lodge that is painted with the victories I have brought our people.

"I would listen to you sing in the night air of the birds you have seen, the flowers you have picked. I would live this summer in the gentle way of an old man."

"You are tired, Father," Metaha said, feeling his father's weary shoulders. "You should take to your lodge now."

"I am tired, my son, but I cannot rest. There is still the prayer for the hunt to be made. I must chant to the spirit of the buffalo."

"I will help you, Father," Metaha said. "You must teach me the words."

"You are truly a son of the sky, Metaha," Waseta told the boy. "You forget your own fear, your own weariness to help your father. There is a greatness to sacrifice. It is something a chief must know above all things."

"You will lead the warriors again this summer," Metaha said. "You will do it because it is what a chief does."

"Yes, my son," Waseta said. "And when the time

comes, you will lead our people, too. This is written in the sky. The winds sing of it this very night."

"It must wait many summers," the boy said. "You will live a long time, Father, and it will be many moons before I grow strong and tall as you are."

"Metaha, my son, you have walked these valleys since the moment of your birth. You have spent ten summers on the earth. You know much of the ways of our people. Would you take your horse and ride beside me to the hunt this summer? Would you run through my fire and sing to me in the night when I am alone? Would you fill my moments with laughter and stand tall even when the great bulls shake the ground with their thunder?"

"Yes, Father," Metaha said, his face alive with excitement. "Am I then to go to the hunt with you?"

"You are very young, and the hunt demands much of a man. There will be no nights of lying beside your mother in the warmth of our lodge. There is no softness in the buffalo valleys. The chills there can take the spirit of a man away into the night."

"I am not afraid," Metaha said. "I have the true aim with my bow, Father. Even Boltah does not deny me that. I can run with the deer, and my heart is strong."

"Your heart is like the mountain, little son of the sky," Waseta said. "You are like the panther, always reaching into the night, always hunting for what he knows not. And you are bright like the stars, my son. You brighten all who see you. It is this last gift that is greatest of all."

Metaha looked at his father's face. The old chief was smiling in a way that always showed the boy the deep love felt by his father for him. Metaha's shining smile sent back the same message to Waseta, and the two walked together back to the edge of the spirit cliff. There they chanted the ancient prayer to the buffalo spirit.

Buffalo spirit, send power to our bow arms
And make our hearts strong,
For the women and children cry out
For our return.
Buffalo spirit, give us courage
And shield us from danger.
Buffalo spirit, send us your sons
That we may be strong and brave.
May our horses be swift
And our aim true.

They chanted the words over and over until the sun broke the horizon. Metaha then followed his father down the steep trail that led to the village of the Honey Dancers. Waseta was tired, and Metaha felt his father lean on him.

The boy was thin, but there was a strength that could not be seen, a strength from the inside which carried Metaha on toward the village.

In the dead quiet of the morning Metaha listened as his father made the preparations for the hunt. Horses were selected, and weapons were made ready. Soon they would ride to the valleys beyond the hills of Katai to seek the mighty buffalo. The thought of it made Metaha's heart race.

IV

The village of the Honey Dancers was alive with excitement that next day. Many suns had risen since a lone warrior had ridden into the village with the news that the buffalo had returned to the tall grasses. Now at last Waseta readied the warriors for the hunt.

The women and children gathered around husbands and fathers who would not be seen for many days. Some would not return. There were dangers and hardships on the trail, and Metaha remembered strong warriors in their prime who had returned covered with buffalo hides, their silent eyes cold with death.

Metaha thought of that as he gathered his arrows. Waseta had gone to say a final prayer for the hunt, taking Boltah with him to the spirit cliff. Metaha had wanted to go with his father, but he knew better than to ask. Boltah would never have allowed it.

The boy took his arrows and checked them. Each of the flint arrowheads held fast, and the fledges were trim. Only two days before, Metaha had replaced one of the fledges he had damaged on a rock. He put a third bowstring, a new one his friend Topai had made, in his arrow pouch. A bow without a bowstring was of no use on a buffalo hunt.

"Metaha, my son," Tahoa said to him from the shadows. "Little son of the sky, I have brought a gift for you."

Metaha turned and looked at the face of his mother. The old woman's eyes were full of sorrow, and it was clear that many tears had fallen that morning.

"You should have run through the waters in the way of a boy for many summers," Tahoa said to him. "You are small, yet you ride off with the men to the buffalo hunt."

"Mother, it is as it is," Metaha said. "I am the son of Waseta, and Waseta's son must learn the ways of a chief."

"Even your father did not ride to the buffalo hunt as a boy of ten summers," she said.

Metaha looked into her eyes. He was close to his mother in a way few boys of the tribe were. Most boys left the arms of their mothers forever when they were very small. But if Waseta had longed for a son, Tahoa had also. The boy who would one day be chief of all the people made the old woman proud. Metaha had learned courage and wisdom from his father, but the gift of tenderness and understanding had come from Tahoa.

"Mother, I will miss you," Metaha said. "I fear I will not return to you as the boy you know this day."

"You will not return as a boy, little one," Tahoa said.

"This saddens you?" Metaha asked, not understanding. Most of the women looked forward with

36

much gladness to the day when their sons would face the terrible ordeals of the manhood trial.

"Metaha, only the spirits write what is to happen on this earth, but I have seen many men ride off to the buffalo hunt. This is not a game to be played at by boys. There is much danger, and only the strongest live to tell of it."

"Mother, you did not see his eyes by the moonlight," Metaha said. "He has grown sad. He needs me. Even if it calls my death, I must go. I owe him my life, do I not?"

Tahoa looked at the brightness in the eyes of her son. Those eyes were filled with an understanding she had taught them. She could feel no more sadness, and she held the boy close to her.

"I will pray to the sky spirits to watch over you, my son," she said. "Now you should have your gift."

Tahoa handed the boy a bright deerskin shirt painted with the signs of the sky spirits. Bright beadwork told of how Metaha had been given to the people by the spirits of the sky as an answer to the prayer of Waseta. It was a brave shirt, a shirt meant for a great warrior.

"It was to have been given to you on your return from the great ordeal of manhood," she said. "It will be too big for such small shoulders. But I have chanted many suns as I chewed the hide, and the beads are from the medicine hills beside the river. You will not wear it yet, little one, but carry it with you to shield you from harm."

"I will, Mother," Metaha said.

The boy then sank his face into the warmth of his mother's side, and she held him close to her. He wanted to stand there forever, but he drew away, telling her with his eyes that the sun would die in the hills many times before he saw her again.

Metaha took his arrows and his clothes and stood beside the lodge of his father. Waseta soon arrived with four of their best horses, and Metaha climbed onto the back of one. Soon the other warriors followed, and the men of the tribe rode off to seek out the buffalo.

When they reached the place of the buffalo grasses, Waseta commanded that camp be made. The blankets were spread, and the drums beaten with prayers to the buffalo spirit. Each warrior sang his own spirit chant. Then they walked naked to the waters to cleanse themselves.

There was a small run of water in that place, and Waseta told his son the spirits had long ago commanded that the men purify themselves before seeking out to kill the sacred buffalo.

"The buffalo spirit sends his sons to us to make us strong," Waseta said. "From the buffalo we make the hides that warm us in the cold. The meat from the buffalo fills our bellies and causes us to grow tall. The sinew we use for our bowstrings, and the horns and bones are made into the tools we use. We show our debt to the buffalo spirit in our prayers, in the sacrifice of the buffalo's heart. We show our worthiness by our dance and by going to the hunt in our brightest paint, washed clean of our toil by the sacred waters."

Metaha joined the warriors in the river. The whiteness of his skin seemed not to belong among the brown chests of the men. Metaha looked at the scars made by lances and arrows and knives in the chests and sides and thighs of the warriors. A man bore the history of his life on his skin, the boy thought to himself.

Metaha's skin bore no scars. His body was still that of a boy, and his arms and legs were thin. He could hear laughter from the young men as they looked upon him, but he knew the day would come when he would stand tallest among them all in the eyes of the people. No man was born tall, and the days of growing were endured by all.

In the night the warriors gathered beside the fires to hear the ancient tales of the buffalo. Kahato, the oldest of the men, began the story with the tale of the first buffalo hunt.

That was in the days before the horse. Then the Honey Dancers were but a small people. Many children died in the cold of winter, for the deer were never enough to keep all the bellies full. The buffalo came only once to the river then, and the warriors prepared themselves by cutting their arms and chests so that the blood flowed. They took no food. Their sacrifices were rewarded by the sky spirits, for the buffalo always came.

The warriors would walk out onto the prairie and light great fires. The fire would rush toward the river, turning the land black. The buffalo would run from the flames as if chased by the spirits of the sky. The earth would shake with the thunder of their hooves, and clouds of dust would darken the sky.

The warriors would scream and beat their drums,

causing the beasts to run faster. Then when they reached the cliffs, it would be too late for the herd to stop. Many buffalo would rush over the cliffs and fall to their deaths in the rocks below. The warriors would then climb down the cliffs and take the dead creatures back to their camp.

It was a dangerous thing. If the fires did not blow toward the river, the buffalo herd was lost. Worse, many warriors would find themselves burned to death. But it brought meat to the lodges and made the people strong.

Kahato, the old man, finished telling this story with a look of pride on his face. Kahato's father had been there in the time before the horses.

It was Nagai who told the next story. Nagai was a tall warrior who had been to the hunt since the time Waseta first led the Honey Dancers as chief. Nagai spoke of the day when the great chief, Katai, first brought horses to the village.

It was in the prime of Katai's manhood, his twenty-fifth summer. He had been to the spirit cliffs to ask the sky spirits to protect the people from the iron heads. That night Katai had a great vision. He saw a four-legged soldier running across the buffalo valleys. This soldier had an iron hat upon his head. When the sun had crossed the sky, an eagle flew above the earth with the iron hat in his mouth. From the dust of day came forth the head of a beast.

Katai followed his vision into the land where the iron heads camped. He came upon four-legged beasts and led them away. That same day the Honey Dancers returned and killed many of the iron-heads. Katai had the soul of the horse from that time, and the Honey Dancers had ridden across the prairies in their numbers ever since.

Metaha listened as other warriors told stories of heroism. He heard the famous story of Katai's battle with the iron-heads on the river that cried. That was the battle when Katai was shot from his horse. The chief wandered across the battlefield, killing many enemies. When he found himself cut off from the others, he cried out to his horse. The beast came to his aid.

When all the stories of the past, all the tales of Katai and the iron-heads and the great white buffalo and the great battle against the blue-shirted white men, had been told, Metaha followed his father to their sleeping place. The boy had seldom slept in such an open place, a place where there were no trees and no lodgepoles. But there was beauty to the sky, and the stars seemed to chase away the loneliness.

"Father, have you ever wondered why the stars are brightest when there is emptiness in my heart?" Metaha asked.

"Is there emptiness inside you, my son?" Waseta asked. "I never knew a boy more filled with laughter, more filled with the joy that visits life."

"It was only that I was thinking of my mother and my home," Metaha said.

"Then I know this about the sky, little one," Waseta said, touching the boy on the shoulder. "The stars are always brightest against a black sky. It is the way a man must be. When he is called to be the strongest, it is always the moment when it is hardest to be strong. The sky reminds us of this. If a man was always to stand in a group of strong men, he himself would never grow strong. It is the man who rides alone who grows strongest."

"I will always be one to stand alone, Father," Metaha said.

"Why do you say this, my son?" Waseta said.

"It is because of my skin, Father," the boy said. "Those who would will always look to me and say, 'There walks our enemy, the white man.' They will remember the iron-heads and the blue-shirts, and they will say, 'kill Metaha, kill the white one.' "

"This is not our way, little one," Waseta said. "There will always be those such as Boltah who hate you for the whiteness of your skin, for the color of the sky in your eyes. But when you look past their hatred and gaze into their eyes, they will know the trueness of your heart. It would not have mattered to the people if Katai had had white skin. He still would have been a great chief. You will win their hearts, my son, with the goodness that grows inside you."

Metaha smiled at his father. A great light flowed out from his small eyes, and the boy sang. As he sang, the other warriors gathered around and shared the beauty of his song. When Metaha finished, the night bathed the camp of the Honey Dancers in silence, and all was quiet. Morning would bring the buffalo hunt, and there would be few nights filled with sleep then.

V

The buffalo hunt had changed much since the day when the great beasts were chased over the cliffs into the river. Now the warriors rode out in search of the animals in small groups. Metaha rode at the side of his father, proudly sitting his horse as though he had been born there. All who saw the boy matched his smile. The hunt was a happier time because of Metaha.

When at last a great herd was found, Waseta commanded the fastest horsemen to ride out and bring the herd on. He then chose the best of his bow arms to wait for the herd. This last group Waseta stood with, telling his son what would come.

"This is the way my father taught me," Waseta said. "He was taught by his father, and he by the great chief, Katai. We send our horsemen to gather the herd. Then we wait for them. When the buffalo come, we seek out the bulls to kill. We take only the oldest and weakest. In this way the herd remains strong. We do not hunt the young. The young must have their day to grow. This is the way the sky spirits bid Katai hunt the buffalo, and we do it even as he did."

"And where do I stand, Father?" Metaha asked. "I am neither swift horseman nor great hunter."

"You stand as a son should, at my side," Waseta said. "When the beasts come out of the clouds of dust, the earth will shake. There will be those who will run away. But you will not run, little one. You will hold your bow with a firm hand and shoot your arrows into the buffalo."

"The buffalo seems a great beast to kill with my arrow, Father," Metaha said.

"Few buffalo ever died from the flight of a single arrow, my son. We fire many arrows into the buffalo. He bleeds, but we are after him. He runs, bleeding into his mouth. He cannot run forever with so much blood flowing, and he falls. Then we kill him with our lances. In this way I have killed many buffalo."

Metaha smiled at his father. All that was to come, but he wondered if such thin arms as his could launch an arrow that could strike down the mighty buffalo.

For a long time Metaha sat on the back of his horse waiting for the dust to come. Then he saw it.

The sky turned black as night, and the earth shook. It was as when the sky spirits were angry and sent the waters to rush across the land. But this thunder came only from the buffalo, and it served only to prepare the warriors for their game. Soon the first buffalo emerged from the dust, and Metaha watched as the warriors shouted and screamed. The herd turned, and then a shower of arrows flew. More than one arrow found its mark, and the warriors charged after the great bleeding beasts.

44

Waseta's arrows struck an old bull, and it went down quickly. A young warrior flashed his lance, and the first kill was made. Metaha followed his father as the chief rode among the buffalo, riding close so that his arrows struck often.

Metaha pulled his bowstring taut and fired at a great bull. His arrow flew into the bull's shoulder, and the beast shuddered. But instead of racing on with the herd, the bull turned and ran at Metaha. The boy's horse was frightened. Metaha did not know this horse as he did others, and the animal did not calm when Metaha put his small hand on its head. In a moment Metaha felt himself thrown to the ground. There he stood with the great bull buffalo thundering down upon him.

Metaha remembered the words of his mother. She had told him of the dangers of the hunt. He remembered the still faces of the dead brought back from the hunt. He thought to sing the chant his father had taught him, the words a warrior spoke to the sky spirits when he was beginning his journey into the world of the dead. But he had no feeling of fear, no feeling of death inside his youthful heart. He took out his bow instead and notched an arrow.

Metaha watched the bull approach. The beast ran hard, but already blood dripped from its mouth. Metaha prepared to let loose his arrow. The earth was filled with silence, and only the boy and the bull filled that moment. Then Metaha let fly his arrow, and the bull's great head shook with fury. Suddenly its eyes grew still, and Metaha watched the beast crash to the ground beside him.

From behind his back Metaha could hear a rush of

horses. He felt the strong arms of his father lift him from the earth onto the horse beside him. There was a fierce shout from the other warriors, and the hunt was given up for the day. Waseta held his son high in the air, and the warriors shouted their approval of the boy with the bright eyes.

"Never have I seen such a thing," old Kahato said, "and I have hunted the buffalo since the sun was young. To kill a bull with two arrows as a boy! This must surely be a sign from the sky spirits. This is a boy truly marked by the light in his eyes."

Others spoke the same words. Metaha felt a glow from within, and he felt warm in the hands of his father. The warriors rode past him, touching the golden glow of his hair. When the last of them had ridden past, Waseta set the boy down and handed him a skinning knife.

"Now is the time for work, my son," Waseta said. "The meat from this beast will keep your belly full when the cold comes."

"Yes, Father," Metaha said.

The rest of that afternoon the warriors skinned the buffalo. They then stripped the meat and began smoking it. No one was hungry that night, and there was much singing. Metaha worked at combing the hair of the great buffalo hide, and he was pleased when his father brought him the horns from the buffalo.

"One day you will wear these in a great medicine bonnet," Waseta said to him. "For now you will keep them in your lodge as a reminder of the moment you faced death with courage."

"I was not afraid this time, Father," Metaha said.

"My hand was steady."

"I know this, my son," Waseta said. "I watched you. I was fearful for your life, but it was as if you had hunted the buffalo a hundred summers. You faced your enemy and struck him down. This is a great thing."

That night Metaha's dreams were filled with great battles and glory. He killed a hundred buffalo, struck down with a war lance a thousand enemies. It was the dream of a boy, but the dreamer was fast becoming a man, if not in stature, then certainly in the eyes of the others.

As Metaha walked across the camp of the warriors that next morning, his friend Topai sought him out.

"I have not seen you, little one," Topai told him. "You have become a great warrior since the time the sun last rose on our faces."

"I am not a great warrior," Metaha said, a smile spreading across his face. "I have only proved to some that I am a small boy no longer."

"To kill a bull buffalo in his tenth summer," Topai said, laughing. "This is the boy I taught to make bowstrings. Perhaps now it is he who should teach me."

"You have been a good friend, Topai," Metaha said.

"A boy who has no brothers should have many friends," Topai said. "The day may come when you are in need of friends, little one. There are those who would be your enemies."

"Yes," Metaha said. "If my skin was the color of the red earth as yours is, they would find words to fill a hundred songs about my deeds. It is hard to forget

47

hatred, though."

"You are wise to see it, Metaha. There are always those who are blind to the false hearts of others. There is a danger in those who hate you, little one. Be always on guard against them. They are like the snake that strikes in the night. Take care in walking alone when they are about."

"It is a hard thing to have enemies," Metaha said, sitting down beside the water. "I hate no man."

"One who would lead our people must face many enemies," Topai said. "Men will always hold hatred in their hearts for a man who is better than they are. This is something you will grow to understand."

"That is what my father says," Metaha told Topai. "It is always that things will be understood when I am older. But my heart longs to know these things now. I know I am young, but I would know these things."

"Follow the wisdom of your father, Metaha," Topai said. "Trust him always. He was young when his shoulders had to bear the heavy burden of leadership. And when the night chills you and you can find no peace, come to the lodge of your friend Topai. I will tell you stories of the old times, and you will find laughter in your heart."

"And we will hunt deer when the leaves fall from the trees," Metaha said.

"We will ride together to hunt the buffalo many summers. You as chief, and me as great warrior of our people."

It was like that always with Topai and Metaha. The boy brought life and laughter, and the man showed Metaha the ways he would grow to know as a man. Topai had only completed the ordeal of manhood three summers before, and even now he looked still like a youth to many warriors. In his seventeenth summer he stood a head short of Waseta, but there were many who were no taller at the end of their growing time.

The warriors hunted the buffalo for many days. The moon was born again in its fullness before the men returned to their lodges. Many buffalo had been taken, and there would be food for all throughout the cold days of winter.

Metaha's return was a great event. He wore a great buffalo cloak across his thin shoulders, and all who were there remarked that he had the look of Katai in his eyes. The sun danced across his forehead, causing his eyes to sparkle and his hair to shine. It truly looked to all as if the spirits of the sky were present in the soul of the boy.

Tahoa was not so pleased that her son had killed such a great enemy. For a small boy to do a great thing meant that he would be small no longer. Already there was talk of the ordeal of manhood in the lodge of her husband, and she cried to think that the small one, the voice that filled their lives with laughter, would soon be gone.

To Metaha she said nothing. To Waseta she said nothing. But in the morning when the birds were in the sky before the sun, she walked to the river and said her own prayer.

"Spirits, do not take my son so soon," she said. "Give me more summers of laughter to my life. I have borne pain and suffered enough in my days upon this earth. Give us only four more summers of Metaha's boyhood."

But as Metaha's fame spread through the tribe, it grew less likely. He seemed to age with each setting sun, and the people longed for the day when he would lead them as their chief. Women felt blessed by the sky spirits when they touched his golden hair, and small boys gathered around him to hear his stories of the buffalo hunt.

When Topai could be persuaded, the two would ride together into the hills to hunt. Each time Metaha returned with some new hide to show his skill, and with the killing came new courage and confidence.

"Already he speaks as a man," Tahoa said to Waseta. "I fear one day soon he will stand up from his blankets as a man grown tall and strong. For if he is the gift of the sky, perhaps he is enchanted. Perhaps he is not a man at all."

"There is too much of this talk among the old women," Waseta said. "He is a boy yet. You have tended his needs. He sat on your knee and wet himself. You have mended the tears in his arms and legs as you would a torn shirt. You have cut the hair back from his eyes. Do you now wish to tell me these things are not things done for a boy?"

Tahoa smiled at his anger.

"Do not hurry him into a man, my husband," she said. "You have years enough left for him to grow old in his own time. The ordeal of manhood is a grave task to be accepted. Even those who are as swift and strong as Topai reached their fourteenth summer before beginning it. You yourself stood the test when you had walked these lands fourteen summers, and there was need of a new chief."

"He will have summers of youth left to him, Ta-

50

hoa," Waseta promised. "But we knew when first we took him into our hearts that he would never be only ours. It is as my own father must have felt. A child belongs always to his people, but a future chief more than others."

"I pray he will be strong enough to be that chief," Tahoa said.

"My wife, if you only had seen him standing there, naked but for his breechclout, with a buffalo thundering down upon him. I have seen brave warriors shake. But he raised his bow and held the string taut with his thin arm. Then with the breath of the beast upon him, he brought its death with his single arrow."

"I have listened to the story, Waseta," Tahoa said. "I have heard it many times. But I fear for him. He spends too many moments in the loneliness of his own thoughts. He does not run through the waters with the other boys. He gives us the brightness of his smile, the joy of his laughter, but I fear he finds no brightness, no joy for his own heart."

"It is the way with chiefs," Waseta said. "His joy will be found in the greatness of his people."

"Yes," Tahoa said.

But to herself she mourned the fact that one so small should walk in such tall footsteps.

VI

Tahoa's words rested heavy on the mind of Waseta. The old chief spoke often to Metaha of passing fewer days in the solitude of his own company.

"These are the men who you will one day lead to greatness, my son," Waseta said. "You must lead them now, also. For it is the loyalty forged in youth that will stand the trial of hardship."

"Yes, Father," Metaha said. "I understand."

But though he tried, Metaha found himself out of place in the boyish games of the others. He who had shot the buffalo in his tenth summer could find no thrill in the trapping of a field mouse or the shooting of a prairie hen.

One morning as he set out for the river with the other boys, they came upon a small deer who bore the signs of a broken leg. She walked on but three of her feet, and it was clear to all that she would soon fall victim to a wolf or panther.

"Let us kill the deer and take it to our fathers," said Lakadai, the oldest. "It will prove to our people that we are great hunters."

"Yes," agreed the others. "Perhaps then our fathers will let us hunt the deer in the days to come."

"What manner of hunter is Lakadai?" Metaha asked, stepping out from the group. "Is it a great hunter who kills the weak and defenseless?"

Lakadai scowled at Metaha. Lakadai had always felt anger for the way the boy with the golden hair was set above them all.

"You do not wear the markings of a chief yet, Metaha," Lakadai said. "Go back to the lodges of your father so that the old women may touch your hair and be favored by the sky spirits!"

The other laughed with Lakadai, and Metaha frowned.

"We are taught that each creature is given to the earth by the sky spirits," Metaha said. "To take the life of a single creature when there is no need is to anger the spirits. We have no hunger in our bellies. This deer offers no danger to our people. It is a wrong thing to take its life."

"Metaha," spoke Retapo, son of the great warrior Ytalo, "we have not gone to the buffalo hunt as you have. We have not killed the great bull with our arrows. Our fathers' eyes are not filled with the wonder of our deeds. We only wish to please them."

Metaha looked into the eyes of Retapo. They spoke with a truth that could not be denied.

"This is so," Metaha said. "But it is not likely that we would fool our fathers with this creature. A broken leg is not a thing that can be hidden. Will we not look foolish to bring to them a crippled creature that we have struck down? Will it not prove to all how weak we are to bring to our people such a creature?"

The other boys sighed. They turned to Lakadai, the oldest. Lakadai drew out his arrow and notched it in his bowstring.

"You will not take the life of this deer," Metaha said, stepping between Lakadai and the animal. "You have heard my words. Do you not see the truth that rests in them?"

"I grow tired at the mumbling of babies," Lakadai said.

"Lakadai, hear me," Metaha said. "If it is Metaha that fills your heart with hatred, then strike him down this day. It will be a small thing to hide the body of one so small. My father says I will one day lead our people in battle. If I cannot lead you this day, then I will never lead you to battle where the hardships are great and the weaknesses many.

"My father has taught me to lead with wisdom and courage, but such things are only seen by a man's eyes," Metaha said. "What is felt in the heart is much greater. Strike me down if you will. But if you can look upon my face as a friend, then take my hand. Together we will find a greater proof of your skill in battle."

Lakadai is said to have drawn the bowstring taut. For minutes the air was filled with silence as Metaha looked upon the moment of his death. Then Lakadai relaxed his hand, and the arrow fell to the ground.

Metaha took Lakadai by the hand. Together they bound the crippled leg of the deer and set it to run into the woods. It was called a great thing by some of the boys, but Metaha remembered it as the day Lakadai was bound to him in friendship.

Later that day Metaha approached the council of

Waseta and sat in the place he was accustomed.

"Do you wish to speak in my council, Metaha?" Waseta asked, noticing the strange urgency in Metaha's eyes.

"Yes, Father," Metaha said. "I ask a thing, not for myself but for my friend Lakadai."

"Lakadai?" Waseta asked. "Lakadai is but a boy like yourself."

"Lakadai does not wish to remain a boy in the eyes of his people forever," Metaha said. "He asks to go to the hunt. I have hunted many times in the thickets across the great waters, my father. There is little danger there, but many deer are known to run across the meadow there. Give Lakadai and me your blessing to hunt the deer. We will bring back a creature to show the people the skill of your sons."

"Why does Lakadai not come forward to ask this?" Waseta asked. "Is he faint of heart?"

"He granted to me the honor of speaking to the great chief of the Honey Dancers," Metaha said. "He is here."

Lakadai stepped forward, trembling slightly in the presence of the chief.

"Lakadai, you will stand the ordeals of manhood when the spirits of the sky ordain it," Waseta said. "Why do you wish to seek out the deer with my son? Why do you wish to hurry the passage of time?"

"I only wish to please my father and my people," Lakadai said. "I would have him think of me as more than a boy fit to run through fires and carry the wood for our fire."

"And, you my son?" Waseta asked Metaha.

"I am bound to Lakadai," Metaha said.

"Is it a bond fairly forged?" Waseta asked the boys.

Metaha and Lakadai glanced at each other, then nodded.

"Then you may go to the thicket," Waseta said. "But you must go with a warrior. Is there a man here who would waste a day of his life with foolish boys?"

Metaha looked along the line of grim faces. Not a man stepped forward. Then he felt a great hand on his shoulder, and the voice of Topai filled the air.

"I will go to the thicket with them, Waseta," Topai said. "I am not so old as to grow tired of their talk, and I have a hunger for fresh meat myself. We will bring back venison for the bellies of all who would have it."

"It is to be the boys' hunt, Topai," Waseta said. "You are only to guard against the panther who lives among the rocks beyond the thicket."

"It will be their hunt," Topai said. "They will have their chance."

"Then go, my sons," Waseta said to the three of them. "Pray to the spirits of those you would strike down. Heed the words Topai might say to you. He is no less a hunter than I."

"Yes, Father," Metaha said, speaking for all of them.

The other boys were envious of Metaha and Lakadai. Others sought to go, but to take many men on a hunt was to risk killing a friend. Topai led the boys across the river alone, and soon the three of them disappeared into the trees.

As they entered the thicket, Topai held back, letting the two boys lead the way. Metaha walked forward, keeping his head low so that little could be seen of

57

him. For many moments the boys waited for some sign of deer. Then, as the sun began its long death into the hills, Metaha motioned to Lakadai.

"There, beside the water," Metaha whispered.

Lakadai nodded his understanding, and the two boys notched their arrows. Then in a single movement the two arrows flew through the air, driving their points into the side of the deer.

For a moment the deer staggered. Then it dipped its head so that the right antler touched the earth. Finally the animal fell on its side, breathing heavily.

"We must end its life," Metaha said, preparing to let fly a second arrow.

"Metaha, my friend," Topai said, stepping forward. "That is not the way. Would you fill his hide full of arrows? Take my lance and bring his death with grace."

"This is better," Metaha agreed, taking the lance. "Lakadai, do you wish the honor of the kill?"

Lakadai took the lance and walked forward. In a moment he was upon the deer's dying body. Metaha watched the deer's mournful eyes look upon them. Blood trickled from the buck's mouth, and a stillness filled the air.

"Make his end swift, Lakadai," Metaha said. "He has earned as much."

Lakadai raised the lance and plunged it deep into the heart of the deer. A second later it was over.

"I have taken my first deer," Lakadai shouted. "Soon I will be as a man."

"A man kills always with a sadness upon his heart, Lakadai," Topai said, taking Metaha's hand. "A man who kills with gladness angers the spirits."

"The spirits would not have us starve," Lakadai said. "Surely they rejoice to find courage in our hearts."

"That is for them to say, Lakadai," Topai said. "You have much to learn."

"He will have the time for it," Metaha said. "Come, Topai, do not spoil his moment. He has waited a long time for it."

Lakadai smiled for the first time at the face of Metaha. A new friendship had been sealed. Topai still frowned, but Metaha was filled with gladness. And whenever Metaha's face was filled with laughter, Topai could not frown long.

"Well, little one," Topai said, laughing. "You have your deer. Now how shall we return to the camp of our people with the meat I promised they would eat this night?"

"We can build a travois and place the animal upon it," Lakadai said.

"You would take the body of a creature struck down in the field to our camp? You would pollute the sacred waters with blood?" Topai said angrily.

"We must dress the meat here," Metaha said. "In this very field. I have dressed the meat from deer many times. It will be no great doing."

"This is a better plan," Topai said. "The meat must be your gift, little ones. I will build the travois where the waters can be crossed. You must bring the meat and the skin across."

"We will do this," Metaha said.

Topai walked away, and Lakadai and Metaha took out their knives. Soon the boys were busy with the skinning. After that Metaha showed Lakadai how to take the meat. It took most of the light that was left from the sun to finish the stripping of the meat. It was in darkness that the boys and Topai at last bore the travois of meat into the camp of the Honey Dancers.

The meat was cooked upon the fires, and the warriors cried out in wonder at the two boys who had killed the deer. It was not such a thing for boys to kill a deer, but a man's first kill must always be celebrated, and the people were glad of the fresh meat.

As the people ate, Metaha bore the deerskin to Lakadai.

"You will want this for a fine new shirt," Metaha said. "Beads can be made from the reed that grows beside the river."

"Half a skin will make a vest worthy of a warrior," Lakadai said. "Then the other half will be yours."

"It was your kill," Metaha said.

"Both arrows struck true to their aim," Lakadai said. "Mine was the kill only because you granted it to me. It is a kill shared. The skin must be shared as well."

Metaha smiled brightly. It was a wise judgment. Lakadai was a friend true to his word. Metaha took out his knife and cut the skin down the middle. Then Metaha handed Lakadai the two halves for his choosing.

Lakadai smiled now, too. The older boy took the smaller of the two halves and handed Metaha the other. As they walked away from each other, Metaha knew that here was one who could be depended on.

VII

Metaha was never so alone among the other boys after his hunt with the boy Lakadai. Though Lakadai was older and half a head taller, it was always Metaha who led, who was expected to lead. And when Lakadai followed willingly, the other boys felt no anger at following, too.

Waseta noticed the new power in his son's face. The arms were still thin even for a boy, but Metaha had the heart of the sky spirits, and it made the boy strong in a way different from others. Waseta knew and understood that it was such strength that brought a chief greatness and made his tribe plentiful and prosperous.

It was during the time of the great cold that the strangers came. It was not unusual for warriors from other tribes to enter the land of the Honey Dancers, but these men came in peace. Their weapons were left behind, and only their great white buffalo robes set them apart from the Honey Dancers.

Waseta greeted them in the tongue of their fathers, a strange language known to but a few of the Honey

Dancers. Metaha marveled at the men. They were taller than even the great chief, his father Waseta. They wore strange shiny bracelets on their arms and hats made from the fur of beasts Metaha had never seen. Around their necks hung shiny pieces of bright metal.

Metaha had heard talk of such men. They came from a land far to the north where the buffalo blackened the prairie. These men fought great wars against the Comanches and the Kiowas, the fierce tribes beyond the spirit cliffs. It was said that one of their chiefs had taken the life of seven Comanches in a summer not far past.

"Metaha, my son," Waseta said to the boy, shoving him forward at the guests. "These travelers have ridden many suns to sit in council with me. They are the chiefs of a people from a land where rivers greater than the waters beside our camp flow. Their lands fall in the shadow of mountains that swallow the sun when there is light for many moments. They are known as great hunters, warriors of great courage. They come to us in search of peace with the Comanche and Kiowa, our neighbors."

Metaha's eyes grew wide. The Comanches were never very peaceful, and the Kiowas were little better. Only the Caddos and Wichitas were peaceful. It had been many summers since the Comanches had made war on the Honey Dancers, that was true, but it was because the buffalo were plentiful, and because Waseta had killed many of their warriors during the last Comanche raid.

"My son, bow to these men," Waseta said. "They are chiefs, all of them. They come to us without weapons in the spirit of friendship."

Metaha bowed once to each of the three men. The boy's eyes sparkled with excitement, and the chiefs were surprised.

"He is born of the white man," one of the chiefs said, speaking in the tongue of the Honey Dancers.

"There is a story to it," Waseta said, leading them into the shelter of his lodge.

While the chiefs ate and drank, Waseta related the story of the time when Metaha was first found and brought to the camp of the Honey Dancers. The chiefs sat stone-faced, smiling at Waseta's words. No one told a story like the old chief, and his guests were pleased. When Waseta told of the buffalo hunt, the visitors smiled at Metaha.

"It is not a small thing for one so small to kill the buffalo," the chief who spoke the tongue of the Honey Dancers said. "I walked the earth fifteen summers before I first killed the great beast. Perhaps he is sent by the spirits."

The chiefs then touched Metaha's hair and held him close to them. Metaha felt the strength in the arms of the three chiefs and was pleased. Peace with the Comanches would only come from strength.

The sun set on the camp of the Honey Dancers that night amidst much singing and dancing. The guests were entertained by the games of children and the wrestling of the warriors. It was a time of much cold, but the laughter of the people brought warmth to the hearts of all.

When the sun rose, Waseta took the arm of his son and motioned for the boy to follow. Metaha was puzzled. Surely Waseta would sit in council with the three strangers this day. Metaha had been to many places with his father, but he had never sat in the council when important things were being said.

Metaha slung the great buffalo cloak around his shoulders and followed his father out into the morning air. A winter's chill froze the ground, but that was the way of winter. Winter was the time of cold, the time of hunger and fevers. It was the time of the children's tears and old people's deaths.

"Father, where do we go?" Metaha asked as they hurried along.

"To council, little one," Waseta said, pausing to explain. "It is because of the chief of the strangers. This man asks that you be there."

"And you, Father?" Metaha asked.

"It is time that you learn the ways of the peace council," Waseta said. "One day it will be you who sits in my place. It is always wise that you learn the ways of the man you must follow."

Metaha walked beside his father the rest of the way to the place of council. A fine roaring fire burned in the council ring, and the three strangers were already seated on one side. Waseta sat on the second side with Metaha beside him. The third side of the council was empty. No one represented the Comanches or the Kiowas.

Waseta turned to the strangers. There was a solemn look on the old chief's face that Metaha had rarely seen. At last one of the strangers, the man who spoke the language of the Honey Dancers, stood and began speaking.

"I am known to my people as Black Raven," the chief spoke. "I am chief of the Cheyenne people. We

64

ride to this place in search of a peace long absent from the valleys of our fathers. For many summers we have hunted the buffalo and killed the sons of our enemies, the Kiowa and Comanche. But in the last moon of summer our people found a greater enemy in the white-skinned men who came over the trails with their great moving lodges.

"These men bring guns, sticks that spit fire and stop the hearts of our warriors. Also the Pawnee move into our hunting grounds, killing the buffalo that feed our children. We have too many enemies. There is a wisdom to putting aside our war lances. Why should we fight our brothers when the white devils kill our young men?

"You wish peace with the Comanches?" Waseta asked. "Why do you not go into the council of their chiefs? Why do you not speak to them?"

"We have fought for many summers against the warriors of the Comanche and Kiowa. Many of their young men have spilled their blood in battle against our young men. I hold the scalp of the son of the Comanche chief. I have raided his horses. I have taken his daughters. There can be no riding into his camp."

"There can be no peace with you," Waseta said. "The sun does not stop because we ask it of the sky spirits. It is not enough to wish peace."

"Then tell us what we must do," the Cheyenne chief said.

"Metaha, my son," Waseta said. "What would you wish of the Cheyenne if you were Jafalo, chief of the Comanches?"

Metaha shook at the mention of the terrible Comanche chief. The stories of Katai had never brought to the boy's dreams the horror that Jafalo's face sent.

"Jafalo is not a man of peace," Metaha said. "But he is a man and would surely have love for his daughters. If they were sent as a gift to their father, perhaps Jafalo's heart would warm to you."

Black Raven stood and walked to Metaha. The Cheyenne chief looked into the deep blue of the boy's eyes.

"There is wisdom in your words, little one with the bright eyes, but it is a grave thing. Jafalo's daughters are given into the lodges of proud warriors. These warriors will not give up their wives willingly. And there are children. The women will not give up sons without many tears."

Metaha looked up into the eyes of his father, but Waseta looked away. The Cheyenne chief wished an answer, and the boy sighed.

"My father has taught me the price of war is great," Metaha said. "But there is a price to peace as well. You must give up the daughters. If they will not go, they must say this to their father. The children must go with their mothers. This is a great price to pay, and Jafalo will feel this in his heart. His present to you will be the peace you long for."

"This is too high a price, little one," Black Raven said sadly. "There will be many deaths before such a thing is tried."

"My friend," Waseta spoke at last. "The wisdom in the words of my son cannot be fought. Jafalo will never make peace while you hold his daughters and grandsons. You must send the girls. If they would return, perhaps Jafalo will give them to their husbands to seal the peace.

"There is also the matter of the scalps. You must send them in a bag of deerskin to Jafalo, the scalp of his son apart from the others. Show that you do not regard the scalps of Comanches as trophies of war. Show you feel only shame for the blood of your brothers shed in battle."

"I will send my own son," Black Raven said.

"Ride back to your people, Black Raven," Waseta said. "Return with the daughters of Jafalo and their sons and daughters. Return with the scalps of the dead. When the moon is full, we will sit in council here again. I will send your words to Jafalo. If peace is in his heart, he will come."

The three strangers stood solemnly and took the medicine pipe from Waseta. Each chief in turn took the pipe and puffed the tobacco. Then Waseta smoked the pipe, sealing the agreement.

In the passing of the suns that followed, Metaha forgot about the council to come. But soon he missed his friend Topai.

"Father, what has become of Topai?" Metaha asked one time when the morning was bright and good for hunting.

"Topai has ridden into the land of the Comanches," Waseta said. "Topai will bring Jafalo to our camp."

"Is such a thing wise?" Metaha asked. "Jafalo is like the hawk. He hunts. He does not spend his moments in council with chiefs of other tribes."

"It was you, my son, who first spoke of the daughters," Waseta said. "I myself have daughters. I would ride into the camp of another tribe to see them."

"You also have a son," Metaha said. "Would you also ride to a council with the man who killed that son?"

Waseta's face became white. For a minute the old chief trembled. At last he sat upon a rock and replied.

"Metaha, my son," Waseta said, "no man ever had such love for a son as I have for you. But a chief is the leader of his people, and all the Honey Dancers are my children. To prevent another man's grief I would speak peace with my enemy. It would be a time filled with tears for me, but it would be a time I would speak of peace. I would break my war lance."

"And Jafalo?" Metaha asked.

"Jafalo grows old," Waseta said. "An old man loves to feel the hands of his grandsons upon his knee. An old man loves to see the smiles of the young, not the grief of the widows."

"Then he will come?" Metaha asked.

"Jafalo has always known war," Waseta said. "Perhaps his heart is hungry for peace."

When the moon came to be born again, Topai led a group of rugged warriors into the camp of the Honey Dancers. They were led by the stern-faced Jafalo, the great white-haired chief of the Comanche nation.

At that time there also came many horses from the north. These riders were the Cheyennes. Black Raven took his place across from Jafalo in the council, and the fire burned bright. The daughters of Jafalo came, carrying their sons and daughters in their arms.

"Jafalo, great chief of the Comanche," Black Raven spoke. "I bring to you the daughters I have stolen away. They bring their children that the light of their smiles may make your heart warm with the glow of peace."

"Those who have been taken away are restored," Jafalo said. "This is as it should be. But there is still my son to be considered."

"I who have taken the life of your son stand before you," Black Raven said. "It is a thing that weighs heavily upon my shoulders. He was young and brave. He should have known many summers."

"You did not mark his body in the way a Cheyenne often does," Jafalo said. "But you took his hair."

"Many scalps have been taken," Black Raven said. "They no longer hang from our lodgepoles."

The Cheyenne chief then passed the bags of scalps to Jafalo, but the Comanche chief seemed unmoved.

"If the scalps were to be seen by my people, there could never be peace," Jafalo said. "The spirits of the dead would cry out for revenge, and there could be no quarreling with the spirits of the dead. It is best that the scalps be placed in the earth where they can call out no more for war."

"This will be done," Black Raven said, motioning with his hand to one of the other chiefs to bear away the scalps.

"Nothing now remains in the hands of the Cheyenne that belongs to the Comanche," Jafalo said. "Nothing now stands in the way of peace. But tell me, Black Raven, does anything remain in the hearts of the Cheyenne that would bring us to battle again?"

"There are always those who would seek battle," Black Raven said. "There are those who enjoy the taste of blood, who call out to the night for the glory sunrise will bring. But there is no glory in the death of our people, Jafalo. And it is that death that comes from the land of the great river."

"The white man?" Jafalo asked.

"He comes like the locusts of summer," Black Raven said. "He carries the sticks that speak with fire. He sends the cowardly Pawnee into our villages to kill the children. He drives the buffalo from our valleys, leaving our bellies empty."

"This holds much truth," Jafalo said. "It is a fool who steals his brother's horses while the forest burns his lodge. There will be friendship between our people. We will seal the bargain."

Waseta took out the pipe and passed it among the chiefs. It was then that Jafalo saw Metaha. The Comanche chief stood.

"Who has brought this son of a white man into our council?" Jafalo demanded. "This is surely a council cursed!"

"This is my son, Metaha," Waseta said, standing up in front of the Comanche chief. "It was his words that first softened the heart of Black Raven. He was sent by the sky spirits to me to share the time of my old age."

Jafalo turned to Metaha and stared hard at him. The Comanche chief slapped Metaha hard across the chest, knocking him to the ground. There was a stir in the council, but Metaha sprang to his feet. Staring with cold eyes at the Comanche chief, Metaha spoke.

"It takes little courage to strike a boy," Metaha said, his fearless eyes chilling all who saw them. "This is the council of my father, so I excuse the ill manners of his guest. It seems foolish, though, to make an ally of the Cheyenne and an enemy of the Honey Dancers all in the same moment."

Jafalo was surprised by the boy. Never before had the old chief been so challenged by a young one.

"Is this the boy who the warrior Topai spoke of, the one who struck down the buffalo in the summer of this childhood?" Jafalo asked. "He speaks with a tongue of fire. I am glad that there is no war lance close beside him."

Jafalo laughed, but the laughter was not shared. The others at the council frowned, and Jafalo still felt the angry gaze of Metaha upon him.

"Bright eyes, forgive him," Black Raven said. "He does not understand."

"I need no Cheyenne to speak for me," Jafalo said.

For a moment Metaha feared the peace would break down at that moment. Then Jafalo laughed again. In a moment the old chief vaulted the fire and took Metaha in his huge arms.

"This is a face to be remembered," Jafalo said. "It was a gentle face, too gentle a face for a chief. But now I read the anger that would lead him to battle against his enemies. This is a sign I search for among brave people."

The old Comanche held Metaha into the air for all to see. Then he set the boy on the ground beside Waseta and probed the depth of Metaha's bright eyes.

"They say there is a mark the spirits put upon a boy," Jafalo said. "I see it in your eyes, bright one. You would find yourself welcome in the camp of the Comanche. I will pray to the spirits that you may live long. May you have the greatness your father's shadow casts upon you."

No one had expected the chief of the Comanches to open his heart to one so small. It was a thing that was sung of around the fires for many moons. The Comanches and Kiowas gathered with the Cheyennes for a great council in the land where the sun dies, and peace filled the prairies of the great rivers. Those who were there say the chiefs touched the head of the bright-eyed son of Waseta to seal the peace and bring the good fortune given by the sky spirits to them.

VIII

That same winter Metaha encountered the second great danger of his young life. It was during the moon of the great snows. White powder covered all the earth, and the animals went hungry. The plants were bent over with layers of ice, and the Honey Dancers were glad of the stores of pemican made after the buffalo hunts of summer.

Each night, fires were kept close to the horses that they might be kept from freezing. No warrior could be expected to spend his nights keeping a fire burning, so the task was turned over to boys.

The nights were long, and Metaha found himself missing the comfort of his father's lodge. The fire kept him warm, but there was no one to share his laughter, to listen to the stories he told of Katai or of the night he stood in the council face to face with the great Comanche chief, Jafalo.

It was on such a night that Metaha's eyes watched the fire kept by Sytago, the small brother of Topai. Sytago, who was brought into the world of light the same summer as Metaha, had always been small.

Like Metaha, Sytago had always been laughed at by others.

Some shared the duty of keeping the fires, but no boy came to help Sytago. Because of the many kindnesses shown Metaha by Topai, the little son of Waseta had always liked Sytago.

Sytago's name meant child of the willows, and it was said that he had been found by Topai lying on the stomach of their mother. Sytago's mother had died in the moment of his first breath, and he was thought to be ill luck by some. Metaha remembered Topai saying there was a fire behind Sytago's eyes, though, and more than once Metaha had known the boy as a loyal friend.

On that night Metaha saw the boy sitting close to the fire. Sytago had no buffalo cloak, only an old deerskin coat given him by Topai. The cold could always be felt through such a coat, and Metaha grew sad at the thought.

As Metaha watched the fire of Sytago he first heard the movement in the trees. He thought for a moment that it was but a stirring of leaves in the harsh wind, but other sounds came, too. There was a scratching against the bark of trees, and a low growl rolled through the air.

Sytago sprang to his feet, drawing a small knife as protection against the danger. Metaha also rose to his feet, cautiously picking up his bow and notching an arrow. The boy's fingers were numb with cold, though, and the bowstring was coated with ice.

Sytago stood before the fire, searching with his eyes for the beast that had filled the night with its sound. It was Metaha who first saw it.

Metaha cast his eyes above Sytago at the limb of a tall tree. There, creeping along the limb, was the most dreaded of the night creatures, the mountain panther.

"Above you, in the trees!" Metaha screamed, racing to the side of his friend. "Be watchful!"

Sytago moved back beside the fire, but his feet were not so quick as they would have been on a summer day. He stumbled, and the panther was upon him, tearing at the flesh of his arms with its jagged teeth.

Metaha pulled his bowstring taut and let fly an arrow. The arrow flew through the cold air and struck the panther in the hind leg. A terrible scream of pain followed from the creature, and Sytago rolled away from it.

Metaha now faced the panther alone. The chill moonlight held the cat in its glow, and Metaha watched the terrible green eyes of the panther fix him in their frightful gaze. Then the cat leapt forward, and Metaha notched a second arrow.

It was as if the panther knew what was within Metaha's heart, for it stilled as the boy pulled his bowstring taut.

"I will bring your death, creature of the night," Metaha said softly. "It is not my way to kill, but if you would seek to fill your belly with the meat of my horses, I will strike you down."

The panther growled deeply. Metaha studied its face. There were hunger and pain there, and Metaha's heart mourned the knowledge that he would bring more pain to the beast.

"This is not like the moment of killing the buffalo," Metaha said to himself. "This is not a creature I must kill to feed my brothers and sisters, my mother and father. This is a life I take with no gladness in my heart."

But it was not to be. The panther let out a great roar, then disappeared into the thick brush. Metaha rushed to the side of Sytago, lifting the boy off the ground.

"Are you hurt badly?" Metaha asked Sytago, feeling the limpness of his friend's body.

"I am only shaken," Sytago said.

But the wounds were real. Many jagged teeth marks covered Sytago's arms and shoulders, and blood ran across Metaha's clothes.

"It is but a short walk back to the camp of our people," Metaha said. "I will take you."

Sytago was hurt, but the boy did not forget his duty.

"There is the fire to watch, Metaha," Sytago said. "You must seek out the others first."

So it was that Metaha brought his friend into the camp of the Honey Dancers only after the fires were left in the care of others. Metaha carried Sytago to the lodge of Topai, calling out in a loud voice to the young warrior.

"Topai, there is danger in the color of your brother's eyes," Metaha said, shaking the sleeping young man's shoulder. "You must attend to him."

"He belongs in the lodge of my father," Topai said, sitting up. "Why do you bring him here?"

"You must know what to do for him," Metaha said.

"It is well, little bright eyes," Topai said, taking his brother from the arms of Metaha. "How were you able to bear him from the fires? You are little bigger than he is."

Metaha stood up and faced Topai.

"There is always strength when the need is there," Metaha told Topai. "These words are your own."

"I remember," Topai said. "Now help me with him."

Metaha and Topai stripped the torn clothes from Sytago's body. Then women were sent for to tend the wounds. Boltah arrived to chant over Sytago, and Topai drew Metaha aside.

"Your eyes are bright," Topai said. "Do you feel the need of sleep?"

"No," Metaha said. "My hand is steady."

"Then walk with me, little one," Topai said. "Bring your bow. We go to kill this panther. It has preyed too long on the flesh of our people."

"It is very dark, Topai," Metaha warned. "The cold covers the earth like a blanket. Bowstrings grow stiff, and there is a swiftness to this creature. It knows the night as I know the river. Killing it will be no easy thing."

"All this is true, little one," Topai said. "But it has felt the sting of your arrow this night. When the sun rises, it will know no fear of man, only pain and hatred."

The two of them walked alone through the darkness. Their only light was the bright moon of midwinter. Metaha had always felt a closeness to the moon. It was the moon that brought light to the lonely darkness, the moon that seemed to smile especially to him. If he had been brought to the earth by the sky spirits, surely the moon must be his brother.

Metaha said a brief prayer to the moon. He prayed for light to see the eyes of his enemy. He prayed for the strength to stand the test Topai had brought him. As the night grew darker in the midst of the tangle of underbrush, he prayed that his eyes might look upon the morning sun.

It was not a long time before they came upon signs of the panther. White bones of beasts killed not long before sparkled in the moonlight. Heads of deer and rabbits, squirrels and raccoons, that had not been swift or sly enough were scattered along the dimly lit trail. Metaha breathed nervously, but Topai walked as if he had been born to hunt the fierce beast in the dead of night.

It was one of the things about Topai that Metaha always found to admire. Topai always walked with his shoulders broad and strong. Topai was a man who could be followed. Topai accepted all that came without tears or complaint.

Soon the two warriors, the man and the boy, came upon a rocky place. From deep within the rocks they heard the deep growl of the panther. That growl had a deadly, cruel sound to it. The noise seemed to peel the skin off Metaha's neck.

Metaha remembered the deadly claws, the jagged teeth, the evil eyes of the beast. It would not be quick in dying, and much blood waited to be spilled. The boy followed Topai, moving to his right as Topai commanded.

They were soon in the rocks, and the growls grew louder. There was grave peril now, and Metaha held his arrows ever ready.

Topai carried a war lance. Its blade flashed in the light, and Metaha knew the hands that held it were the hands of a true hunter. Soon the point of the lance would lie buried in the heart of the panther, Metaha thought to himself.

They did not have time to think of things now. There was a sound to their left, and the panther emerged from the rocks, his hind leg still bleeding from the arrow embedded there. Metaha notched his arrow and pulled his bowstring taut, but Topai stepped in front of him.

"Panther, great creature of the night," Topai called out. "You who would strike at a boy keeping watch in the night, hear me! I am Topai, warrior of the Honey Dancers, who has come to end your life. I will be the one to see the suns of many more summers. You have seen the last of your life!"

The panther seemed to understand the words. The beast flew through the air at Topai. Topai tried to spear the panther with a jab of the war lance, but the cat was too quick. In a moment the panther had escaped the lance of Topai and was racing toward the trees. That was when Metaha let fly his arrow.

Metaha remembered taking his arrows to the spirit cliff to be blessed by the sky spirits. This arrow must surely have been charmed, for it caught the corner of a rock and drove itself into the body of the panther.

The creature turned once more. Blood filled its mouth, and there was a smell of death in the air. Its evil eyes held Metaha in their gaze, and the deep growl that pierced the air was meant for Metaha alone.

"I will put the finish to it," Topai said, stepping forward. But the panther moved first.

"Metaha, strike hard at it!" Topai screamed as the panther raced at the boy.

79

Metaha dropped his bow and pulled from his waist a great knife given to him by an old warrior who had hunted with Waseta. The panther flew through the air, but Metaha moved aside. Then, with a single movement, the boy opened up a great gash in the belly of the panther.

The creature's growl stilled. It landed in the brush beyond Metaha's feet, its eyes closed by death. Topai held Metaha up in the air and cried out to the sky spirits.

"See what the little one has done, spirits of the sky!" Topai screamed. "See what the small hand has laid low! See that Metaha has killed the evil creature of the night, the murderer of man and beast! He has closed forever the eyes of the most evil of creatures!"

Metaha felt the earth shake. A great thunder spoke from the heavens, and flashes of lightning lit the sky. There was a feeling of power in the boy's shoulders, and he left Topai's arms and walked to the dead panther. The chill left the air, and Metaha warmed with a great pride.

"Spirits of the sky, I thank you," Metaha said. "You have kept me from the harm this creature brought. You have returned me to my village, to the lodge of my father. May you ever walk at my side in time of trial."

The skies cleared, and Topai took the tail of the panther.

"They will worry," Topai said, leading the way back to the camp of the Honey Dancers. "There will be many songs sung around the fires of the Honey Dancers about this night, little one. Many warriors will tell of you on lonely nights in the buffalo valleys.

80

You who have touched the spirits of the sky with your words will one day be a great chief of our people."

"Will the day come when you will follow me into battle, Topai?" Metaha asked. "You are a leader of warriors, not one to follow."

"I would follow you, little one with eyes that sparkle with the light of the sky. It is a thing commanded by the sky spirits. To follow is often a hard thing, but to follow courage is never so hard. They will all follow you, Metaha. They will stand at your side in battle as you lead them to greatness. And I, Topai, will be forever at your side."

"Yes," Metaha said. "Always the bravest and wisest of all."

"Of those who follow," Topai said, smiling.

Many songs were sung that night. Many tales were told by the light of the fires. It is the way of a legend to be born in the feat of courage. So it was with Metaha.

IX

The sun rose and set many times. In the passage of that time Metaha grew tall, strong. He came to lose the look of a boy and take on for the first time the posture of a man.

The signs were many. His chest was broadening, and the fat had left his thighs and middle. His shoulders became like the rocks of the river, and his arms were thin and frail no longer.

Metaha was the tallest of the boys who walked through their fourteenth summer. His bright eyes and golden hair marked him as one who was different. Still the old women reached out to touch his hair for luck, but now the children huddled around him in the evening to hear the stories of his courage. Warriors came to test the strength of his bow arm, and other boys challenged him in the wrestling circle.

All this was not lost on Waseta. The old chief grew proud in the knowledge that his son was already one known for courage. In the days since the council of Jafalo, Metaha had grown in judgment, too. It was the answer to Waseta's prayer that the boy should be what he was.

Waseta smiled at the thought of his son leading the warriors to the buffalo hunt. He smiled when he saw the arrows of Metaha fly swiftly to their destination. But there was a sadness, too. Soon the laughter, the gentle music of his singing, would be gone forever from the lodge of Waseta. The old chief knew the time for him to live would not be many moons after his son's voice was absent from his lodge.

It was during the first moon of summer that Metaha and Waseta traveled alone to the river. The great trials of manhood would soon begin, and each father at that time took a son approaching manhood to the river to see if it had come to be the time of his test. As Metaha ran through the waters beside his father, Waseta grew warm in the shadow of the boy's laughter. As they took fish from the water to fill their bellies, Waseta thanked the spirits of the sky for their gift of gladness.

It was when the sun was setting in the sky that Waseta told Metaha of the ritual. Metaha had heard of it from Topai and others older than himself. It was the dedication to the sky spirits. The boy would wash himself in the waters of the great river in the company of his father. If the spirits chose this to be the time of the boy's manhood trial, the father would know.

Mataha did not know how the spirit chose a boy. His father had never brought him there before. Some boys came many times, waiting until their sixteenth or seventeenth summer to undergo the trials. But such boys were always small, and Metaha was already above the shoulders of Topai.

"There is a prayer to be said when you walk into the

waters, my son," Waseta said. "It is to be a prayer from the heart, but it should speak to the sky spirits of the time of manhood. You must ask always to be chosen. When you return from the waters, I will know."

Metaha stood before the river and stripped himself. He felt foolish standing naked in the twilight. Boys ran naked through the camp of the Honey Dancers, but Metaha did not feel like a boy. As he walked into the waters, he chanted a prayer.

Spirits of the sky, my fathers,
I give myself up to you.
You who bring the sun and the moon,
Who bring to us the buffalo to fill our bellies,
Who command the wind and the rains;
I, Metaha, son of Waseta
Cry out to you that this may be the moment
Of my manhood.
My bow arm is strong
And my heart you know to be true.
My eyes see the true way,
And I will keep always the sacred rites of my people.
I stand here ready to serve my people,
To stand before you as a warrior.
If your eyes take pleasure in what they see,
Let my father see the mark of manhood upon me.

Metaha walked proudly from the waters. As he emerged from the water, his father's face was filled with sadness. Metaha frowned. His chest was broad, his bow arm strong. He seemed to be and feel like a man to be.

"I see the sadness in your eyes, my father," Metaha said. "I have failed to bear the mark of manhood."

Waseta took the boy in his arms and held him close.

"You read what is upon my face, Metaha, but it is I who have borne falseness. The mark is there, my son. The sadness is that of a foolish old man who would share the laughter of his son through many more summers."

"You will always share my laughter, Father," Metaha said, looking up into the eyes of his father. "There can be nothing to keep my songs and stories from your side."

"There can be only one thing," Waseta said. "That thing which always comes in time. You must understand, my son, that soon you will face the ordeal of manhood. When you return from your quest, you will take your own lodge. Soon you will find a life to share your laughter. There will be a life for you away from my eyes and ears."

"That can never be," Metaha said.

"My son, it is the way with life," Waseta said. "The spirits of the sky make it so. It is the way a man grows. To deny it would be an unnatural thing. Go forward in pride, my son. Never look back to the days when you were but a boy. Sing no more of the past. Live only for the day to come."

"Father, I do not wish to go so soon. There are those who go to their manhood test much later. This is but my fourteenth summer. Another summer will do as well."

"Metaha, you have wisdom in your bright eyes. Do

not you know this is a thing commanded by the spirits of the sky? It is not a thing chosen by you or me. It is a thing that must be, just as the rains fall and the winds blow. You who have never stood back in fear of man or beast must not now hold back from the greatest challenge of all. Go forward, my son, to stand alone as a man."

"I will do this, Father," Metaha said. "Who will tell my mother?"

"She will know," Waseta said sadly. "She will see it in our eyes. She will not misread them, my son. She will know the thing as it is."

Metaha dressed slowly, then followed his father into the village. Already the drums beat with the news that others bore the mark of manhood. The boys Lakadai and Heturu were marked as well. Both were older than Metaha, and much was made in the village of one so young bearing the mark of manhood.

As they had done many times before, the old women touched his hair. Songs were sung beside the fires, and Topai and others came to celebrate the proudest moment in a boy's life. Metaha laughed and clasped the hands of the warriors as they greeted him as one who would be a boy no longer. But in another place there was no laughter.

Tahoa had known from the eyes of her husband that the mark of manhood was upon their son. She sat on a rock and wept for the last of the warm days that would come to their lodge.

"Do not weep, foolish woman," Waseta said to her. "Our son will soon take the place he came to us to take. The gift the sky spirits sent was not meant for us alone. It was a gift destined for all the people."

"He has grown tall, my husband," Tahoa spoke, "but his spirit is still that of a boy. He runs with the wind, and his arrows fly with the true aim, but his heart still belongs to you and to me. He is not a man yet. He hurries himself to the hour of the challenge."

"He is strong as the others, Tahoa," Waseta said. "His legs have grown powerful like the panther. He has the heart of the great buffalo, and there is a quickness about him that brings to heart the rattlesnake.

"You have always seen the way he walks the earth. There is an understanding of the land, a communion he shares with the spirits. No beast holds anger in its heart for him. He is a gentle boy, and he will make a kind and thoughtful man. This is your doing, my wife, and the people will prosper for it."

"I will miss his softness, Waseta," Tahoa said. "I will miss the touch of his small hand, the feel of his cheek against mine. I will feel empty in the absence of his bright eyes. We will live always cold and alone without the warmth of his laughter, the sunshine of his smile."

"It is a thing to be done, Tahoa," Waseta said. "A woman bears two great pains in her lifetime, the pain of childbirth and the pain of giving away her son to the world of manhood."

"I never felt the pain of childbirth with Metaha," Tahoa said. "Perhaps this is why the pain I feel now is so severe. My husband, I feel a terrible third pain also, the pain that is brought by the death of a son. This pain I have much fear of."

"He is strong and wise, Tahoa," Waseta said. "The ordeal is a thing that must be faced, and he will face it. He will go off from our sight, and we will walk with heavy thoughts. But he will return with the feather of the eagle and make us proud."

Tahoa smiled faintly.

"It is a thing that cannot be helped," she said sadly. "I will pray for him."

"Yes," Waseta said. "Pray that he is strong and of courage. Most of all pray that his eyes see with wisdom, for the greatest peril is always that which is unseen."

When Metaha came at last to the lodge of his father, Waseta took him into the woods to speak to him. The chief told of the ordeals of manhood. Metaha knew them as well as anything a boy could know, but he listened with reverence.

"Metaha, my son," Waseta said. "There is a power to your arms and strength in your heart. These are given to you by the spirits of the sky, the makers of all things. The strength they give you must forever be a gift. Do not forget that we are always but like the pebbles of sand in the river of time. It is but a little thing for our life to end."

"Yes, Father," Metaha said.

"When the sun next sets, we will stand on the spirit cliff and pray to the sky spirits to bring you wisdom in your trial, to give you strength to pass the test and heart to bear the pain. There is much to be done, my son, but I do not fear for you. You have the mark of a chief in your eyes, and the gentleness with which you touch life will make you precious to the sky spirits."

Metaha started to leave, but the hand of his father drew him back.

"Metaha, my son, you should have had many suns

to lie in the lodge of your father," Waseta said to the boy. "You should have felt the gentle touch of your mother many summers. The spirits hurry you to manhood, for they look upon the face of an old chief and know there is never time for the young to grow slowly."

"You will lead the buffalo hunt for many summers," Metaha said. "Soon I will ride at your side, a war lance in my hand. Our spirits will be as one, you and I. We will make our people fierce and proud."

"This will come to pass," Waseta said, clasping the hand of his son to his chest. "I will pray for you in the hours you are parted from my side."

"And I will carry myself to my trial with the honor you have taught me, Father," Metaha said.

That night was warm, but a chill swept through the lodge of Waseta. There would never again be such warmth there as had been before. There would never again be the glow of smiles or the ring of laughter.

X

Metaha followed his father to the top of the great spirit cliff the next morning. The skies were dark and violent, and a harsh wind swept their hair back. Waseta took out his knife and cut open his arms. The letting of blood as a sign of devotion was a thing done often by men of strong medicine, and Waseta did it that day in honor of his son.

"Spirits of the sky," Waseta spoke solemnly. "Look down upon the earth and bless my son, Metaha, who you brought to me that our people might grow in power and numbers. Guide him through his hardships and protect him from harm. He is of the true heart, and his eyes hold wisdom."

Lightning flashed behind them, and Metaha's nerves became raw. The spirits seemed angry.

"Hear me, spirits of the sky," Waseta spoke again. "I leave my son here before your eyes to speak to you in the way most solemn."

Waseta drew Metaha out to the edge of the cliff and told him to bare his chest. The boy removed his vest. Next Waseta removed the leggings and deerskin boots from the boy's feet. Last of all the old chief bore away the boy's breechclout, leaving him bare before the spirits of the sky.

"It is wise to show yourself to the spirits in this manner, my son. Naked we are born to this life, and naked we always stand before the spirits. Would you give of yourself to the spirits?" Waseta asked, handing the boy his knife.

Metaha took the knife and cut into the soft flesh of his chest. Bright red blood oozed out, trickling down his stomach and across his thighs.

"I am as nothing to the power of the sky spirits," Metaha said, remembering an ancient prayer his father had spoken many times. "All that I am is but a shadow in the light of the sky. See how the blood runs from my chest. Life can come only from the heavens. A man may gather greatness to his heart only if he is favored by the spirits."

The boy then felt the wind sweep across his chest. The blood was blown away, and his long golden hair was flung upon his face. There was a moment of silence, and then the clouds seemed to speak to him:

"Metaha, son of the brightness, go out and seek your destiny. You who are strong of heart must bear much in the days to come. Be strong of heart, little son of the sky."

When the wind passed, Metaha walked back to his father and smiled.

"The spirits spoke to my heart," Metaha said. "I will be strong and wise in the hour of my challenge. Father, I will not disappoint you or the sky spirits."

After dressing himself Metaha walked alone from the cliffs. His father remained to pray for the other boys, Heturu and Lakadai.

Metaha spent the last moments before the time of challenge alone beside the rocks of the river. It was a place where he had played, where he had spoken to the spirits in his childhood. It had always been a place where peace could be found.

That day he spoke to his heart, gathering the strength and courage he would need in the days to come. He felt the power in his arms, and he knew that his legs could carry him over the mountains and across the valleys. It would only be the loneliness that would be hard to bear.

When Metaha returned, the three boys who were to accept the challenge of manhood were taken to a small clearing outside the village. There they were told to ready themselves for the tests to come.

Every boy knew the three tests of manhood: the trials of weapons, of fire, and the great ordeal. There were many ways of making oneself ready, and when Metaha looked around the clearing, he saw that weapons had been left there to be used in practice.

"I have no fear of the trial of weapons," Lakadai said to Metaha. "My arm is strong, and I have thrown a lance many times. But I have seen much pain on the faces of those who have returned from the trial of fire, and there are those like Batara who do not return from the ordeal."

"Yes," Metaha said. "But there is no training for the ordeal. The time is best spent with the lance and war ax."

"This is true," Heturu said, agreeing. "I have been told the war ax should always be thrown first. It is the lighter of the two and must be thrown with perfect

93

balance. The lance is a weapon meant to be thrown. The war ax is rarely used in this way by our people."

The three boys spread out and began throwing the weapons. Heturu was right about the war ax. It was a heavy weapon, and it didn't fit well in the small hands of youths. Lakadai's hands were big enough for control, but the tall boy could not discover the secret of the weapon's balance.

Heturu had little luck, either. The war ax had to be thrown downward, and the small boy had trouble managing its flight.

Metaha did better. Many times he had thrown the war ax of his father, and he knew the tool could best be controlled with a short quick movement of the hand. Metaha's war ax began striking the trees regularly, and the others stood in awe.

"You seem to do it with such ease, Metaha," Lakadai said. "It is like you were notching an arrow and shooting it through the heart of a deer."

"Heturu spoke of it already," Metaha said. "The secret lies in the balance. If the weapon is thrown with speed, then it will bite into the tree and hold. But if the handle or the head of the ax strikes the tree, it will not bite. It must strike with the blade."

"Yes," Lakadai spoke. "But I do not seem able to do this."

Metaha showed Lakadai the quick stroke. Then Lakadai held the ax behind his ear and threw it with great strength into the trunk of a tall tree.

"You must show me now," Heturu said. "Show me how to hold it."

Metaha took Heturu's hand and helped it grasp the feel of the war ax. At first the war ax was foreign to

Heturu's hand. The handle of the weapon did not seem to belong to the hand. Then Heturu came to understand the feel of the ax, the balance. By the time the sun stood straight up in the sky, all three boys were driving the war ax into the tree.

Metaha only threw the war lance four times. It offered no challenge to the son of a chief. Metaha had thrown Topai's lance many times, and his shoulder was strong with the power needed to drive it into a tree. Not once did the lance fail to hold its place in the tree.

While Heturu and Lakadai practiced with the weapons, Metaha took off his boots and began running amidst the sharp rocks and briars of the clearing. The other boys marveled at the cactus spines and briars that hung from the flesh of Metaha's feet, but still the boy ran on. When at last Metaha sought the shade of a tree to rest, the others ran to him.

"Why do you torture yourself?" Lakadai asked. "Is this a sacrifice to the sky spirits?"

"No," Metaha said.

"Then why do you abuse yourself so?" Heturu asked. "Your feet are torn by rocks and cactus, and blood covers your toes. Is this good for a man's spirit?"

"Only in the way that it helps me become a man," Metaha said. "It is a thing I heard from Topai. He told me of the trial of the fire. He said a boy is made to walk the ground between two long fires. This ground is hot, and many feet are burned. But feet made tough with scars do not burn as feet who have known no hardship. My feet will be ready for their challenge."

The other boys understood, and soon all three of them ran across the rocky ground. Afterward, herb mixtures were made to ease the pain that night.

After the sun died in the hills, a strange silence filled the clearing. Darkness swept through the place, and the boys laid themselves upon the hard ground to seek slumber. As they lay there, Metaha heard the soft song of a small bird. The bird sang in a way that delighted the boys, and Metaha whistled softly back to it.

"There are those who say you speak with the spirits, Metaha," Heturu said. "Is this so?"

Metaha turned to the boy and looked puzzled.

"I would not say that I speak to them, Heturu," Metaha said. "It is only that I feel what they feel, understand what it is they speak of in the night. I know the soreness in the feet of a horse or the joy in the heart of a small bird. Such is nothing to be looked at with surprise. It is but the way of things."

"I do not feel what the bird feels," Lakadai said. "I cannot walk among the horses as you do. They know you, Metaha. When I go among them, they grow nervous. My father says it is a mark that you are son of the sky."

"That is the talk of old women," Metaha said. "I do not know the man and woman who bore me into the world of the light. I know but the mother who nursed me, the father who took me to his heart. They are known to you. If my heart speaks to the creatures, it is perhaps because for many summers they were all I knew to talk with. I was shunned by many for the color of my skin and the brightness of my eyes."

"That was in the time of no understanding," Lakadai said. "My father hates the white men for the many deaths they have brought. But I have never seen you angry, my friend, only willing to give to those who need the gift. This is the way of Katai, the great chief. Some would say the spirit of Katai fills your heart."

"These are words that make a man proud," Metaha said. "But there is little truth to it. I am but a man like you. I seek but to do what I can manage."

"You can manage anything, Metaha," Heturu said. "I have seen you hunt with the bow. Your arrows fly as if they had eyes. There is a calm that fills your face in the moment of greatest danger. One day we will ride to battle together. I will be one eager to follow where you lead us."

"I, too, will follow you, Metaha," Lakadai said. "This you have known for many summers."

"Yes," Metaha said.

As the boys slept in the clearing, they were startled by sounds in the night. Terrible screams and growls and animal noises filled their ears. Lakadai took up his war lance, but Metaha stilled his hand.

"It is only the warriors come to test us," Metaha said.

"They do not sound like the cries of men," Lakadai said.

"Their voices are bold, my friend, but I do not read the spirits of beasts there. It is only our fathers come to chase the calm from our dreams," Metaha told them.

The voices of beasts filled the night with their cries. Lakadai and Heturu shivered with fear, but Metaha slept with the calm of a man at peace with life. He knew that not to rest was a sure way to fail a test of skill or strength.

For three days the boys worked with the weapons and raced through the clearing, scarring their feet so that they bled. On the fourth night the beat of a drum split the silence of the evening, and the warriors came upon the clearing dressed in the clothes of battle. Only their war paint was missing.

The warriors came for the boys each in turn. Heturu first, then Lakadai. Finally Metaha, too, was borne away. The boys were bound so that they could not speak or hear. Their clothing was set aside. Then they were taken to a place known only to the warriors where boys were dedicated to the spirits.

"Hear me, great spirits of the sky," spoke the chief priest Boltah. "These who come to spill the blood of boyhood are given to you with our prayer. As they are marked for manhood, let your eyes be upon them."

Metaha shuddered as a great silence flooded the place. He felt someone clip a lock of his hair, then press a sticky paste into his mouth. His head began to spin, and he felt a numbness come to his body. Then a piercing scream shattered the silence, followed by another. Finally Metaha felt a sharp pain, and he screamed out into the night.

XI

Metaha woke to find himself lying in the clearing once again. The other boys sat up beside him. They, too, shook the clouds from their heads. Metaha was confused. He remembered nothing but a stabbing pain. Looking down, he saw that he bore a strange mark on his thigh. Blood had dried on his leg, but he could see the mark was the sign of the sky. He remembered seeing a mark of the same type on the thigh of his father.

"Do you have a mark on your thigh, Metaha?" Lakadai asked, limping to his friend.

"I have the mark of the sky," Metaha said. "My father has such a mark."

"Mine is the mark of the river snake," Lakadai said. "I also have seen such a mark before, on the thighs of my father and brothers. It is a family mark. I never before knew how it came to be there."

Heturu also had a mark. It bore the shape of a charging buffalo. It also was a family sign.

"It is the mark of manhood," Metaha said. "Now we will never again walk through the camp of our fathers as boys."

"This is so," a voice from behind the clearing spoke. "You have now been dedicated to the spirits. Your lives as men soon begin."

The boys were startled by the voice. It seemed to have a hollowness to it. It was as if there was no body behind it.

"Soon a warrior will come to speak to you of the trials of manhood," the voice spoke. "You will now come to a time where you must join the world as men or go forth forever from the valley of your fathers."

The three boys stood up, confused. They found water with which to wash the blood from their legs. Then they dressed themselves and waited for the warriors to come. It was not a long wait, for soon three warriors walked through the clearing, each taking a boy by the arm and leading him away into the woods.

It was Topai who came for Metaha. The little son of the chief was surprised to see his friend. But when Metaha smiled and started to speak, a solemn look from Topai silenced him. Topai then took his hand and led him to a place of quiet in the woods.

"You have begun your journey into the world of men, little one," Topai said. "What has passed so far is a thing of little danger. What will follow will bring great peril."

"I was fearful when they put the knife into me," Metaha said, smiling.

"You speak still as the boy who ran at my side through the camp of our fathers," Topai said. "This is not the time of speaking. You must bear what I say with much thought. Silence should fill your spirit."

Metaha looked deeply into the serious eyes of Topai. Then the young warrior began speaking.

"It was in the time of Katai that the marking of manhood began," Topai said. "It was thought that each man should have a spirit to guide him through the world of light. So it was that the mark is made on the thigh where it can be seen as a warrior rides to battle. Such a sign brings to mind that a man is marked forever by the spirits that would guide him. The mark is passed on to the sons of a man so that the son may be mindful that he has a debt to his fathers.

"There are two other marks of dedication. The first is the gift of a lock of hair to the spirit of fire. The hair of boyhood is a sacred thing to the spirits, for such hair brings with it the glow of innocence. Before your ordeal the last hair of your childhood will be removed."

Metaha remembered seeing Topai and others as they had set out on their ordeal. The hair had been clipped from their heads before they left, marking them as candidates of the ordeal.

"The second mark is a simple thing," Topai said. "It comes of the spirits themselves. It is the first sign of manhood, the mark your father saw when he took you to be cleansed in the river."

"I did not notice such a mark, Topai," Metaha said.

"It is not a thing to be noticed by a boy," Topai said, laughing. "You have walked many days as a boy. Do you not see what has come to mark you as a man?"

"But that is not a thing that came to me when I was in the river," Metaha said. "It is a thing that has been

101

for many days."

"It is the thing your father saw," Topai said. "It is why he took you this summer to the river. He saw the look of a man about your shoulders, the new tones in your voice, the hair that has grown about your body. These things you did not have before. They mark you as more a man than a boy."

"So now I begin the trials of manhood," Metaha said.

"I am sent to you to explain the first of these," Topai said. "Of all things in the life of a warrior, his skill with weapons comes first. So it is that you will first be tested for your skill with the war lance and the war ax. Do you have skill with such weapons?"

"I have practiced," Metaha said.

"Can you place them in the trunk of a great tree?" Topai asked. "You will have but one chance. If you fail, you will forever walk in the way of a woman."

"I will not fail if the spirits smile upon me," Metaha said.

"You answer well, little friend," Topai said. "Have you heard of the test of fire?"

"Many times," Metaha said. "In this test I will be made to walk between two great beds of hot coals. The ground will scorch my feet, and warriors will press heated lances into my flesh. I must not scream."

"You have heard much," Topai said. "This trial is to test your courage, the strength of your spirit. In time of battle each warrior is bound to the other. A weak man may betray his people under torture. A strong man will die before he gives aid to his enemies."

"I can bear pain," Metaha said.

"Let me see your feet," Topai told him.

Metaha raised his feet and showed them to Topai.

"You have scarred them on the rocks," Topai said. "I remember when the flesh of your feet was white as the snow of winter. You are now truly coming into your manhood. Soon the marks of lances will scar your chest and side. You will become a different being."

"Is this not our way?" Metaha asked.

"Yes, but it is a hard way on the young," Topai said. "I have spoken to you of the first trials. You will learn of the others from Boltah."

"When do I set out on the first of these trials?" Metaha asked.

"You have two suns for the scars on your thigh to heal. Food will be brought to you as now. Then you will stand your trials."

The two suns passed swiftly. There was much practicing to be done. Each evening Metaha walked to a quiet place and prayed to the spirits of the sky for strength. When it came to be time for him to stand the trials of manhood, he felt strong and sure of his skills.

The warriors came for the boys as the first shadows of darkness approached. They took the boys to a place of great secrecy. There were skulls mounted on poles beside the entrance. Inside was a tall tree painted with the sign of the great spirits of the sky.

Waseta stood before the warriors and told the three boys what they were to do. Each in turn was to take the war ax and the lance and plunge them into the ceremonial tree from a distance of many steps.

Topai carried a war ax and a lance, giving them to Lakadai. The tall boy drew back his hand and hurled the war ax. The air was filled with silence for many minutes. Then the ax caught the corner of the tree and held fast.

Lakadai sighed with relief. Metaha could see the tension ease slightly on the face of Lakadai's father and brothers. To miss would have meant disgrace, banishment or the life of a woman.

Lakadai had little trouble with the war lance. It was thrown with strength into the lower part of the tree. The warriors shouted, and Lakadai was led away from the place of trial.

Heturu was next. Topai brought him the weapons, and the small boy held the war ax tightly in his hand. Metaha said a brief prayer for the boy. The war ax was heavy, and it was no easy thing to send it flying through the air so great a distance.

Heturu swung the weapon back many times. Twice he started to throw it. When he finally did, Metaha could not bear to watch. But the spirits answered Metaha's prayer, and the war ax sliced into the tree. Heturu breathed heavily, then balanced the heavy lance in his hand. The lance weighed down the boy's shoulder, and the faces of the warriors were filled with concern. When at last Heturu threw the lance, it struck the tree low and held firmly in the bark.

Metaha was now the only one left. Topai handed him the weapons. Metaha glanced at the tree, careful to notice where the other weapons rested. Then he prayed to the spirits a final time for strength. A moment later Metaha hurled the war ax dead center into the tree. Before the warriors even caught their breath, the war lance flew through the air and plunged into the tree directly above the war ax.

No one among the warriors had ever seen such a thing. Topai ran to Metaha and held the boy up in his strong arms.

"Such skill with weapons in one so small!" one of the warriors said.

"He must be the son of the sky spirits!" said another.

There was much talk of Metaha's skill with the lance and the war ax. But Metaha could only think of the trials that were still to come.

The boys were led to another place beyond where the ceremonial tree stood. Their eyes saw the two great beds of coals, the red heat glowing in the twilight. Metaha watched as warriors lined the beds of coals and plunged the points of their lances into the fires. Then the boys were led to the head of the line of warriors and stripped.

Metaha watched as fear filled the eyes of Lakadai. An almost helpless feeling seemed to cover the face of Metaha's friend. Then Lakadai began walking.

Pain filled Lakadai's face as he made his way across the fiery ground. Warriors held lances near the boy's flesh, and Metaha could see spots of red appear on Lakadai's arms and legs. But Lakadai never cried out. His groans brought a sadness to Metaha, but Lakadai walked from the column of warriors with a look of triumph on his face.

Heturu approached the warriors next. The small boy was stripped and sent down the line of warriors. Metaha saw smiles on the faces of the younger warriors as they pressed their lances close to the boy's flesh. Burns soon appeared, and small tears ran down Heturu's cheeks. The boy's father showed shame for the tears, but the boy did not cry out. When Heturu stepped past the line of warriors, he collapsed. Warriors carried him to the side of Lakadai, and the two boys dressed themselves.

Metaha faced the trial of fire with courage. He stood still as the warriors removed his clothes. Then he started through the line of warriors.

The ground burned his feet, but the scars dulled the pain. Warriors held out their lances, burning his flesh. Boltah ran the point of his lance close to Metaha's eyes, and the boy had to step close to the fire to get around it. Topai held his lance against Metaha's thigh, and the pain flooded his whole body. Passing Waseta, Metaha wanted to fall into the arms of his father. But Waseta had no smile for his son. Instead the old chief held his lance against the side of Metaha, scorching the soft flesh black as night.

Metaha had never known such pain. Not even the leg that was broken as a boy had brought such anguish. But Metaha did not call out. He held the pain inside himself, praying to the sky spirits that there would be strength to endure.

At last Metaha stumbled past the last of the warriors. Pain was written all over his face, and the burns were such that the flesh smelled of burned meat. Topai took Metaha in his arms and carried the boy to a place where water was kept. The wounds were tended, and the warriors shouted. All three had passed the first of their trials. Soon it would be time for the last of the trials, the greatest test of all.

XII

There was much celebrating that night in the camp of the Honey Dancers. Those who had started the path from boyhood to manhood were feasted. Metaha had never thought his belly could hold so much food. There were prickly pears and buffalo steaks fried with prairie onions. No greater feast had been held to honor the chiefs of the Cheyenne and Comanche peoples.

All around the fires that night men spoke of their own trials. They spoke quietly as they remembered those who had failed the test. Metaha himself remembered one man who had worn the clothing of a woman after failing the trials of manhood. He had not been old in the number of his summers, but Metaha remembered the man had not lived long. He had fallen from a high place and been killed in the rocks of the river.

Many others had died. One old warrior remembered a brother killed by the Comanches during his trial. One warrior recalled with much sadness a young man slain by his own brother during the time of the ordeal. Whenever Metaha asked about the ordeal, though, the warriors spoke of other things.

"This will be told to you by Boltah," they said.

That night Metaha and the others were taken back to the clearing to sleep. They would never again sleep in the lodges of their fathers, but they were not yet men to set out their own lodgepoles. When darkness bathed the clearing in its peaceful shadow, Metaha turned to Lakadai.

"I never feared the test of fire," Metaha said. "Fire is but a thing to be faced. I have felt the pain of fire upon my arms and legs many times. But there is something about this ordeal that chills my soul. It is hard to understand that which is not known."

"Yes," Lakadai said, agreeing. "Metaha, my friend, it is said the hills are covered with the bones of those who have not returned from this ordeal. I have heard my brothers speak of it when they do not know that I am there. There is a great law against speaking of it to one who has not completed the four trials. But I have heard them speak of it sometimes."

"Tell me," Metaha said.

"I will share what I know of it," Lakadai said. "A boy is taken to a place beyond his village. They cut from his head all the hair of his childhood. They then pour dye over his body so that it is baked into the flesh. It remains there until the next moon is born."

"I know of this," Metaha said. "I have seen it many times. The boy may not be seen by anyone while he wears the dye upon his skin."

"He is then given a knife and sent naked across the land," Lakadai said. "There is a quest to be completed, but such is never spoken of. To return alive is no small thing."

That thought flooded Metaha's dream that night. It was during the next day that Boltah sent for them. Lakadai went first, returning without speech.

"You are unwell, my friend?" Metaha asked.

Lakadai said nothing. Fear was upon his brow, though, and it concerned Metaha.

Heturu went next. The small boy also returned in silence. Fear filled the eyes of Heturu, and Metaha could think of no terror that could have brought so pale a color to his face.

It was near darkness when the son of Boltah came to take Metaha to the priest. Metaha was fearful, but he would not let it show. He remembered still the time Boltah had led him into the place where the snakes lived. Boltah was not a man to face with fear upon one's face.

The priest was waiting in a place Metaha had never seen. It was not far from the camp of the Honey Dancers, but a dense woods kept the place from sight. Boltah was dressed in a great red robe of fine cloth covered with the signs of the spirits. Upon his head the priest wore the head of a wolf, a sign of great medicine.

"I have come, Boltah," Metaha said, sitting at the feet of the man. "I am here to listen to what you would tell me."

"You are here to learn the lore of your people," Boltah said. "It is a thing a man must do before setting out upon the ordeal of manhood."

"I open my ears to the words you would share with me, great one," Metaha said.

"Do not mock the spirits by calling a man 'great

one,' " Boltah said with anger in his eyes. "This is not a thing to be taken lightly. From this moment you are sworn to an oath of silence. You may speak to no man until the sun rises upon you again."

Metaha said nothing after that. He listened as Boltah began the long narrative of the Honey Dancers, how the spirits brought the first man and woman out of the river and gave to them the land where the Honey Dancers camped even then.

"Our people were not always strong," Boltah said. "It was in the time of the old chief, Mopau, that the trials of manhood began. The people were weak, and there were times when they were swept from the valley of their birth by others. In that time the Honey Dancers broke the land, grew things in the earth. When the rains did not come, the people were hungry, and the little ones died. Mopau was not pleased. He ordained that the warriors must pass a test of great courage.

"The first two trials you have passed. There are those who would say you are strong, like Katai. But there is more to a warrior than throwing a war lance into the trunk of a tree. More even than standing the heat of a lance point. A warrior must be a man to stand on the high ground when others would remain below. This is why the ordeal is kept silent to all. It is a test of the spirit as well as the arms and legs of a man. It is a challenge to the heart."

Boltah left his place for a moment and walked to a small shelter. From this shelter he brought out a small box. Inside the box was a skull. Boltah placed this skull so that the moonlight danced eerily across its face.

"This is the skull of Nurata, son of Mopau," Boltah said. "The chief's own son was the first to face the four trials. It is said that Nurata drove the war ax and the lance into the ceremonial tree with rare skill. It is said the boy walked the line of fire with great heart. But in the ordeal that followed, he was seen by his father drinking from the waters of the river. To prove that the test was meant to be true, the chief struck down his own son and had his head posted on the gate of the ceremonial ground as a warning."

Metaha remembered how Waseta had pressed the hot point of the lance into Metaha's side. It was much the same.

"Many heads have kept their vigil outside the ceremonial place of our people. Many have died in the four trials. But it has made our people strong in the eyes of all. Our people have never again left the land promised to us by the spirits of the sky."

Metaha watched as Boltah returned the skull to its box and took it back to the place where whence it had come.

"Since the time of Nurata's death, many have faced the four trials," Boltah said. "Your father returned from the trials to lead our people to greatness. It is the trial that forges the strongest of men. A man only grows strong who faces the most difficult of trials. The trees grows strongest whose roots dig deepest for water, whose trunk stands firm against the fiercest wind.

"You have heard of how Katai began the marking of men. This is a thing added to the trials. The pain you felt as the knife bit into your skin is as nothing to the hardships you will face upon the ordeal to come."

Boltah's face held a wicked smile, and Metaha knew the man was laughing inside as he thought of the pain that would find Metaha in the days to come.

"There are two parts to the trial left to you," Boltah said. "The first is known as the ordeal of manhood. When the sun has set three times, you will be taken to a place outside our camp. There you will be stripped naked. Your hair will be cut from your head and given up to the spirit of the fire. A great white dye will be made to cover your skin.

"You will then stand for one day in the path of the sun so that the dye may bake into your flesh. When you are white as the stars, you will be handed a knife and sent upon your way. For the passage of one sun across the heavens no one will seek you. But from that time any man or child who sees you will strike you dead. You have no right to fight such a man. By being seen you give your life to him.

"Others know of the trials. Comanches kill any they see. Caddos will feed you, but you are sworn by the trial to take no food given. You must eat the food you find for yourself; you must not accept the shelter of any man's lodge; you must not take weapons or help from anyone. This is the law of the ordeal."

Boltah searched Metaha's eyes to see that the boy understood. When the priest was satisfied, he continued.

"Much is said of the ordeal," Boltah said. "Boys who set out must never return before the dye is gone. Death is all they will find here by doing so. Three of you will test yourselves this summer. You must take care not to keep each other's company. Such is forbidden by the law.

112

"Each man must seek his own path in the light of this world, and to trust in the smile of another man is never enough to make a man strong. Strength must be sought in the solitude of a man's thoughts, and you will find it beneath an open sky in the silence that flows from the night.

"This is the challenge of the ordeal. You must wait for the color of your skin to return before you seek to complete the last of the four trials. Of this trial you must never speak, not even to your father. A man's quest is sacred to his own spirit. It is not a thing to be spoken of.

"To journey among men a warrior must have strength and courage. But life is not a journey among men. It is a journey among all that love. It is most of all a journey along a path made by the spirits of the sky. To see clearly, a man must seek out the spirits of those who would lead him. A brave quest requires a man to go beyond the world of men. He must reach out to touch the world of the spirits; he must fly above the land and see with true eyes what the world of light would bring him.

"This quest will be your fourth trial. On this quest you will scale a great mountain. You will walk with naked feet across the wide waters. You will kill a creature of the night. And when you have done these things, you will climb a high place and stand before the spirits of the sky. You will speak of what you have done, and you will seek a vision of what will come.

"It is when you finish these things, each in its turn, that you will begin the greatest quest of all. This you will do by walking to the hills that lie between our village and the buffalo valleys beyond. In these hills you will seek out the great hunter of the night, the great horned owl. You will find he is a great enemy, for his claws are sharp and his eyes see when there is no light. Such a quest is only for the bravest of heart, the strongest of arm. Such a quest should fall upon one who would lead our people in the way of his father."

Metaha listened to the instructions of the priest with much attention. The boy searched the man's eyes to see if there was something hidden, something the man had not said. The quest surely held its dangers, but he saw nothing in it that would call for his death. Was not this man the one his father had warned was Metaha's greatest enemy!

Boltah motioned for Metaha to rise. The boy then made his way from the place of secrecy to the river. Metaha climbed slowly up the great spirit cliff and stood alone beneath the great sky. The wind whispered through the night, and Metaha made himself bare as before.

Spirits of the sky, Metaha said silently. I am Metaha, the boy you sent to Waseta to keep his heart warm during the summers of his old age. I have struggled to be as a good son to this man. I have tried to be worthy of what the warriors have said of me. It is not an easy path you have led me to, spirits of the sky. I can walk it only with your help.

Metaha felt the wind touch his shoulders. It was not an answer, but he felt a closeness to the sky spirits.

Spirits of the sky, Metaha said silently, lead me to know the heart of Boltah. If there is a danger in the quest he sends to me, lead me out of peril. My heart holds only love and no anger for any man, but my father is the wisest of all who walk the earth. He is rarely wrong in judging a man's heart.

Metaha stepped back from the edge of the spirit cliff. Something bothered him, but he would find no answers in that place. The answers could come only from the mouth of his father, but Boltah's words echoed through his mind.

"Each man must seek his own path in the light of this world," the priest had said. That much at least of the man's words was true. Metaha knew that to touch greatness he would have to seek his own answers, walk his own path.

He shared the silence with the night a moment longer. Then he started back to the clearing, knowing he would soon lie beside Heturu and Lakadai. But Metaha would not share the peace the others found in sleep. His dreams were filled by the dangers of his quest.

XIII

Metaha felt a hand upon his shoulder in the moment of the sun's rising. He was amazed to find a circle of warriors surrounding him. They drew him to his feet and carried him to a place beside the river. Metaha had watched other boys stand in this place. He stood in silence as the warriors bore away his clothes and left him standing naked in the morning sunlight.

Next an old warrior who was called Jytau approached. Jytau was too old to ride to the buffalo hunt, but the man had a steady hand, and it was Jytau who shaved the hair from Metaha's head.

Metaha swallowed a great sadness as he watched the golden curls of his childhood fall to the ground beside his feet. Warriors gathered the hair and fed it to a small fire.

"This, the sign of boyhood, is given up to the spirit of fire," Waseta said solemnly as his son and the others watched. "May the fires of these warriors burn always with the true spirit of all warriors."

Metaha could feel Jytau's knife cut away the last

117

small hairs from his head. He remembered looking upon the hairless heads of Topai and others.

"Close your eyes now, my son," Waseta said.

Metaha closed his eyes. He felt someone cover his eyes with a cloth as others poured dye over his head and shoulders. Men rubbed the dye into his flesh, and Metaha felt uncomfortable. Their hands were rough and far from gentle. But it was over quickly, and soon Metaha's eyes were open to the light again.

Metaha looked at the strange color that covered his body. It had a haunting glow in the mist of morning, and Metaha found himself feeling strange. Looking at the like figures of Lakadai and Heturu, Metaha saw the same uncertainty in their eyes. It was the last time any of them would face their people as boys.

Metaha was confused by the feelings that filled his heart. For all the summers of his life he had waited for the day when he would stand at the side of his father as a man. Now that day was upon him, and Metaha found himself mourning the passing of the gentle times of his boyhood. He knew there would be no more running through the fires and singing in the night upon his father's knee. Life would be like the lonely times at the buffalo hunts.

All that day the three candidates for manhood stood in the sunlight. The dye cracked and hardened, and the stain was sealed in their flesh. Metaha never moved all the time of that day. Heturu and Lakadai leaned on trees during the heat of the day, but Metaha felt the eyes of his father on his face, and he wanted the chief to see his son was worthy.

In the early part of the day Topai walked to the place and smiled at Metaha.

"Metaha, my little friend, you are a boy no longer," Topai said. "You bring to my heart the picture of a small boy with the head of a rock."

Metaha was trying to stand solemnly, but his heart found laughter at the words of Topai, and a smile crossed his face.

"Boltah will be displeased," Topai said. "He would have you walk to your ordeal with a heavy heart. Remember this, little friend of Topai. There will be solemn days to come. Recall the laughter of your boyhood in such times. This will warm your heart as no fire can."

Metaha looked at Topai with a smile upon his face. Metaha wanted to speak, but Topai walked as a wisp of smoke, and the young warrior was gone.

Others came to the place that day. Many were young boys who came with the questioning eyes of boys. They had seen Metaha and the others many times, and they sought to discover what it was about them that marked them as men.

Metaha remembered how his own eyes had peered at others. There was something comforting about the way life repeated itself. It somehow filled some of the emptiness Metaha felt from the loss of his childhood.

Metaha also felt the eyes of his mother. Women were forbidden to come to this place, but Metaha saw her tear-filled eyes through the branches of a tree. To look at her would have been very bad, but Metaha was sad that he could not brighten her life with a smile at that moment. Such a smile was needed by the face that greeted Metaha's eyes. It would have been but a small thing.

As darkness settled in all around the boys, Boltah

came and led them back to the clearing, where they would await the morning of their ordeal. Metaha found a quiet place beside the tallest of the trees. There he sat alone and thought of the trial to come. The stars moved across the sky, but Metaha's meditation was unbroken. He knew sleep would be hard to find in the days to follow, but his heart was torn by new feelings, and many times he remembered the words of his father.

"A wise man does not walk into battle with a heavy heart, my son. He goes to the place where spirits can be heard and seeks that peace that can be found only in the solemnness of his own heart."

Metaha hung his head and sought to find the answer to his troubled heart. He prayed to the spirits of fire, the spirits of the hunt, the spirits of the river. No answer came to his heart. Then he stood up and looked into the quiet sky overhead.

"Spirits of the sky, help me to find my way in this life. It is said each man seeks his own path in the world of light, but my world is filled with darkness. Send me the light from your stars that I might know and understand. It was never meant for me to remain a boy, but my spirit is not at peace in this time when I seek my manhood. Something unnatural whispers to my soul."

Metaha looked into the heavens and watched a bright star glimmer to him. There are those who would say that the boy heard a voice that night, a voice belonging to the spirits of the sky.

"Walk with pride through the land we created," the voice might have said. "Fear only the false smiles, the false words of men. You will find nothing in the world

120

of our making that would dim the brightness of your eyes."

Whether the spirits spoke to the youth or not is something to be searched for in the hearts of men. But it is known that Metaha returned to the clearing with peace in his heart. No sadness crossed his youthful face, and the passage of the night was filled with a gentle sleep.

Morning held no such peace for the three youths. They were taken before the sun greeted the land to a place beside the river. There they were each given a knife and made to stand facing Waseta, the chief of their people.

"You have come to call your boyhood to a close," Waseta said. "You stand before the warriors of the Honey Dancer people, armed with but a knife and stained by the mark of the ordeal. Do you understand the laws of the ordeal?"

Waseta pointed his war lance at Heturu, and the youth said, "I understand."

Next Waseta held the lance before Lakadai, and the tall youth also said solemnly, "I understand."

When Metaha's turn came, the young man looked deeply into his father's eyes. The eyes betrayed concern and doubt, and Metaha sought to show with the iron stare with which he returned his father's stare that there was not a measure of fear in his heart.

"I understand," Metaha said solemnly when Waseta asked him the question.

"Be warned by our people," Waseta spoke. "May the spirits of the sky watch over your journey from boyhood to manhood. It is no small step to take. You go forth from our people naked as you came into life.

The creatures of the land stand in wait of you. Our enemies will ride through the hills in search of you. Our own warriors would strike you down in the instant they see you. Remember that as Mopau shut the eyes of his son long ago, each man who stands here is prepared to do no less."

Metaha thought he noticed the old chief's lip quiver as the words passed into the air. Waseta then took a small stick and held it up to the light. The first rays of sunlight danced upon the twig, and Waseta held it high for all to see.

"Life is much as the twig I hold in my hands," the chief said. "It is but a small thing to bend it or break it."

Metaha flinched as his father snapped the twig in his hands.

"To be strong a man must grow as the tallest tree. He must probe the earth and grasp the truth with its roots. At that moment he must hold fast, weathering the storms of winter and the trials of man. Even so, he must always yield to that which is stronger."

Waseta then drove a hatchet into the trunk of a tall tree.

"Even the strongest of warriors must bow to the spirits of the sky. Do not let your hearts stray from the true ways of your fathers, my sons," Waseta warned. "Let the honor in your eyes be your guide through the perils of your quest. We now give you up to the world. No man will ride from this camp until the sky has grown dark and light again. Know that any of us whose eyes fall upon you while the mark of the ordeal stains your flesh will strike you down. Father, brother, friend—it will make no difference. The penalty for failing to do so is the death of both. The mark of the trial is upon you. Go each of you in his own way. Go each of you to find the path of your own life. Pray to the spirits of light that they may keep you safe."

Metaha watched as Waseta and the others turned their backs on them.

"We cast out the boy in each of you!" Waseta shouted. "Return to us as warriors. If this is not to be, return never again to the lands of our people. Only death awaits you there."

Metaha and the others then turned and began walking from the lands of their childhood. The way was difficult. Cactus spines pricked their legs, and sharp rocks tore into the flesh of their feet. Metaha walked for a while with Lakadai, sharing the company of the other youth in the hour of their first wandering.

"It is time to go our own ways, my friend," Metaha said at last. "Which path would you take, to the hills or the valleys?"

"I have always found peace in the valleys," Lakadai said. "There is water and food there."

"May you be held in the safety the sky spirits reserve for the true of heart," Metaha said.

"I would say to you the same, my friend, but the sky spirits always walk in your eyes, Metaha. You will be worthy of this trial. I will greet you next as a man," Lakadai said.

"I would have it so," Metaha told his friend.

The two then parted, each beginning a journey into a world of loneliness. Metaha found a great silence filling his life, but as his heart filled with courage, the sounds of the earth came into his ears, and he smiled.

"There is a pleasure in the sound of your voices,

little birds," Metaha said. "It is you who will share my company."

Metaha's feet traveled much ground that day. His shoulders stooped as night fell, and he was weary. Still he did not stop. No man could walk so far in the hours of daylight as a horse could run. Only by walking into the night would he find safety from the warriors who would ride in search of him.

XIV

In the first days of Metaha's ordeal, sleep came rarely. The buffalo grasses stirred with the movement of warriors sent in search of him. One time as he lay close to the earth with the grasses covering him, a horse passed not five feet away. Another time the peace of twilight was shattered by cries of Comanche horsemen.

After three days of running, of hiding in caves and racing through briars, Metaha's flesh was burned by the sun. His feet bore great blisters, and his side was torn by cactus and mesquite thorns. The time had come at last to rest.

Metaha found a small cave covered by the growth of plants and a small tree. There Metaha rested. By the light of morning he wove strands of yucca into a garment to cover his nakedness. The coarse fabric bit into the soft flesh of his stomach, and he found himself remembering the way the deerskin clothing his mother had made for him was gentle to the touch.

In the time that followed Metaha busied himself with the making of snares. As he set out his traps, he discovered a fine area of hard black flint. With his knife Metaha chipped away flakes of the flint and carried it to his cave. Soon he would have arrowheads for hunting.

When Metaha had made seven strong arrowheads, he crept out into the daylight and cut long straight branches from a nearby tree. These he shaped into the shafts of arrows, carefully balancing them so that their flight would prove true.

Next Metaha collected the discarded feathers of birds. These he cut and shaped to form the fledges. The arrowheads he secured with strong twine made with tree bark. He then pasted the end of the shaft with tree sap, completing the fledging of the arrows.

Metaha felt better now that he had arrows, but arrows without a bow were of no use at all. Metaha had made a bow from a tree limb before, but it was no easy task. He found a small willow sapling and tested a branch to see if it was limber. There was a good feel to the wood, so Metaha began the job of shaping it to its task. It was a long and difficult task, but finally the bow took shape.

The bowstring was more of a problem. He stretched many vines, but none of them held their shape. He finally wove bark from a tree into a string, but it would do for only a single shot. Such a bow would hardly prove accurate.

When darkness settled over the land that night, Metaha walked quietly to the places where he had set out his snares. A small rabbit had been trapped in one, so Metaha's belly was filled at last.

Metaha had only eaten rabbit uncooked once before. It had little taste that way, but to risk a fire would be the greatest folly. Such carelessness by young men on their ordeal was the reason the ceremonial grounds were guarded by many skulls.

Metaha's dreams were flooded by many ghosts that night. He saw the face of the old one, Katai, leading his people to the buffalo hunt. Metaha's eyes also saw Waseta as a young man, already tall and strong in the way of great warriors.

Last of all his dream took him on a hunt with his friend Topai. Metaha remembered notching an arrow with his youthful fingers, letting the arrow fly so that it struck a deer in the heart, killing it. Metaha remembered that time with great fondness. It was the first time Metaha had killed an animal.

When Metaha awoke that next morning, he remembered all he had seen in the dream. The spirits often spoke through dreams, and Metaha saw in the dream a message. He would take the bow and stalk a deer that day.

To kill a deer with a bowstring of tree bark would be no easy thing, but a deer would put to an end many of his problems. There would be meat for his belly, deerskin for clothing, sinew for a proper bowstring. Feeling the rough yucca breechclout, Metaha felt a great longing for the softness deerskin would bring to his thighs and belly.

Metaha sat down in the darkness of the cave and put his head in his hands. He sat in silent meditation, remembering all he had seen in the dreams the night before. Then he stood up and looked through the entrance of the cave.

"Spirits of the sky, I have seen the vision you have sent my way," Metaha said. "I walk the land with an arm strong and true. It is to the hunt I go this day. May my aim be true and my bow worthy of the task."

Metaha walked into the daylight and stood still again.

"Spirits of the hunt, of the deer," Metaha called out. "Send to me a deer that I might kill it. It is a thing that must be done. I have need of its meat for my belly and the sinew which would make for me a true bowstring. I seek to take life with a reluctant heart, knowing only my great need makes such a thing worthy."

Metaha stood still for many moments. Then he started into the woods in search of the deer. Metaha's bare feet made no sound as he crept through the underbrush. The air was filled with a warm stillness that brought streams of sweat rolling down Metaha's face and chest. It was not a day to be moving around. Metaha thought for a moment to retreat to the cave, but he knew it was not likely that the warriors of the Honey Dancers would be riding out in search of him on such a day. The dream had come to him the night before, and the spirits might grow angry if he turned away from such a good sign because the sun brought sweat to his brow.

So on he walked, stepping carefully so as to avoid the sharp spines of pencil cactus and prickly pears. His shoulder was torn open by a long mesquite thorn, and he groaned. A thin trickle of blood dripped from the wound, but it soon dried. It was shortly after that when Metaha found the first sign of the deer.

He had seen the footprints of deer many times. Even as a boy Metaha had known the tracks of animals for what they were. The print he found this time belonged to a single deer.

"Perhaps you are sent by the spirits to test me," Metaha whispered. "Perhaps you are like me, sent away by your tribe to prove that you are worthy. Or perhaps you are but a wanderer across the land, belonging to no man or no place."

Metaha spoke no more. He busied himself with the task of tracking the deer. The trail was fresh, and the animal could not be far. But this was a deer that knew the woods, and his trail passed through many places difficult to follow. In the rocks Metaha nearly lost the trail. But the air was crisp, and there was no wind. The smell of an animal lingered, and Metaha followed.

It was said among the Indians of the great rivers that no tribe took to the hunt as the Honey Dancers did. There were many kinds of hunters, but few knew the ways of creatures as the Honey Dancers did. There were no better men to track game, be it buffalo or deer. So it was that Metaha caught the scent of his prey.

The deer soon came into Metaha's sight. It was a tall buck with many prongs to his antlers. His coat bore the marks of many summers, and Metaha knew he was a deer that knew much.

The deer stood in a small clearing beside a pond. Its mouth dipped into the water, but its eyes still swept back and forth in search of enemies.

You are a wise deer, Metaha thought to himself. You seek an enemy unseen. You know only the loneliness of the woods, yet you expect what is not to be expected. This has brought you your long life.

Metaha knew this was the way to live alone. Only

by keeping one's eyes always on guard for enemies did one live to see the suns of many summers.

Metaha now drew his bow out and took a single arrow in his hand. He notched the arrow and started his approach. To kill a deer so strong would take a powerful arm. The arrow would have to fly with great strength into the heart of the beast.

Metaha had no such power in his arm. His bow was true to any task he had ever set upon it, but to kill this deer he would have to be close. Looking at the bow he held in his hand, Metaha knew he would have to be very close.

Metaha was a true hunter, though, and he knew the ways of circling prey. He was like the eagle in search of the rabbit. Though his quarry might move in a hundred ways, the eagle would grasp it with its talons. Such was the way Metaha would kill this deer.

Metaha started by moving away from the animal. The deer seemed to detect a movement, but Metaha froze, and the deer turned away. Soon Metaha melted into the brush, pausing to place a ring of leaves upon his head. Other leaves he tied to his chest and arms. Then he slipped through the woods, moving as the wind does, leaving no sign.

Through the underbrush Metaha moved. Over cactus and through briars he wandered. His legs were scarred a hundred times, and thorns ripped his chest, but he felt no pain. A hunt was never a thing done with ease, and he had often faced hardships seeking the buffalo and deer in the times of his boyhood.

As Metaha made his way around the pond, he felt at last the wind upon his face. His scent would now be hidden from the deer. He now found a small clearing and waited for his prey. He had waited in this manner many times, and only rarely had he failed to find his shot.

The clearing was small, and Metaha readied his bow at the edge of the woods. The shot now would be a thing of ease, and Metaha waited only for the deer to appear. It was a thing that could have taken many moments, but even as he thought of it the deer's antlers moved in the midst of the mesquite trees before his eyes, and Metaha notched his arrow.

The ill-fashioned bowstring grew taut, then slipped on the willow bow. Metaha held his breath as the deer sniffed the air for some sign of an enemy. Then the great antlered beast stepped into the clearing, and Metaha readied his shot.

It is a sad thing to kill such a brave creature, Metaha thought to himself. But it was a thing to be done, and Metaha's fingers slipped away from the bowstring. The arrow flew through the air with a grace Metaha had never imagined. The arrow was true to its aim, and the point pierced the deer's chest and drove through the heart of the animal. Metaha glanced at the eyes of the deer with sadness as its death shrouded the clearing. Then the beast sank to its knees and rolled dead against the earth.

Only then did Metaha look at the broken bowstring in his hands. It was a loss of much labor, but the bow had completed its task. Soon there would be a new bowstring of deer's sinew that would send his arrows upon their way.

Metaha walked sadly to the deer, his heart heavy with regret for killing the animal.

"Old warrior, it is with sadness that I called your

death," Metaha said. "It is only because I need from you the strength you can give me. Your life was brave, and the death I brought to you was a death faced with courage. I honor you at the moment of your death."

Then Metaha made the throat cut to release the blood. Before cutting further, he turned to face the bright summer sky, wiping the smile of triumph from his face.

"I send my prayer to you, spirits of the sky," Metaha said. "It is you who have sent to me the meat that will make my arms strong, the sinew that will make bowstrings to send my arrows on their way. All these things have come from you, great spirits. It is as you showed me in the vision of my night. I will prove worthy of your faith."

Metaha then set to the task of skinning the deer. He prepared a stretching rack and bound the skin to it. Then he left the hide to dry in the sun as he cut away the meat. Metaha imagined a small fire made of dry wood would make little sign in the heat of the afternoon. He built a fire and began the smoking of the meat. As the fire grew warm, he made a pit for the smoking. He buried strips of meat among the coals. The smell filled the air, but little smoke departed into the sky.

Metaha's final task was to cut sinew for bowstrings. The sinews he stretched upon sticks in the afternoon sun. By nightfall Metaha had a bow worthy of any man. Three strong bowstrings had been fashioned, and meat for many suns had been smoked. All this was but the beginning.

From the skin of the deer Metaha cut a fine new breechclout and like leggings. He also sewed moccasins for his rough and scarred feet. With what was left the youth made a band for his head and a small vest. He chewed the hide to make it soft, and he discarded the yucca mat with a great smile upon his face. There was a softness to the deerskin, and he felt for the first time a part of his world again.

That night he slept peacefully. But when morning came, he was reminded by the dye upon his arms and chest that he was still a man hunted by others.

XV

As Metaha prepared to leave the cave that morning, he was surprised to hear shouts in the small clearing below. A shudder worked its way down his spine, and he crept to the cave entrance, peering out at the movements in the underbrush.

The grasses moved, and five horsemen rode into Metaha's sight. Their leader was Boltah, the chief priest. Metaha's old enemy bore a smile upon his face as he pointed to signs that someone had been there.

"You are found, son of the sky spirits!" Boltah screamed, laughing. "You will never see the time of your manhood feast."

Metaha shook with anger as he looked into the hatred that filled Boltah's eyes.

"The hatred I see in your heart, old man, will but make me strong," Metaha mumbled.

"Use your eyes!" Boltah screamed. "He must be near. I can smell the fire of his camp."

Metaha smiled to himself. Boltah did not yet know the fire was but a place for cooking meat. The priest would not be fooled long, though. Metaha knew he must stand ready for the moment of his escape.

Metaha took out his vest and slipped his arms through it. He then covered his loins with the new breechclout and slung his arrow bag over his shoulder. Then he put a sack of dried meat on his back and picked up his bow. Finally he sat quietly and offered a prayer to the sky spirits.

"Spirits of the sky, smile upon me in my time of need. It is my folly that has drawn the warriors to me. I should never have built a fire. I should have walked many miles from this place. Now they are near, and their hearts are full of laughter at the thought of taking my life. Let me have the strength you have always sent to me that I might escape the danger that awaits me."

As Boltah and the others searched the ashes of Metaha's fire, the youth crept from the mouth of the cave and made his way silently among the trees. Boltah urged the warriors on in their search for Metaha, but the others lacked the hatred that filled Boltah's heart. They preferred to talk of the fire.

"He has killed a deer," one of them said. "By the look of its antlers, it was no small beast. He has the eye of a hunter."

"His belly will now be full," another said. "The memory of nights when hunger gnawed at my insides remains with me even now. He will be hard to find."

"Fools!" Boltah screamed. "He must have a camp in the caves. You must search out the place and kill him. I wish to see the face of Waseta when we hand him the head of his son."

The other warriors stared at Boltah in surprise. They held no such hatred for the youth. But they

136

turned to the cliffs and searched for the entrance to the cave. When at last they found it, Boltah rode there and dismounted.

"I come for you, little white man," Boltah said, taking out his war lance. "Soon you will live only in the world of darkness."

As Boltah entered the cave, Metaha slipped by the other warriors and disappeared into the woods. The youth threaded his way through cactus and briars. The sounds of Boltah and the others echoed through the valley behind him, and Metaha left them and the danger they brought to him there.

Metaha walked on, trying to think of a new place of refuge. The caves would no longer be safe. Boltah and the others would search there many suns. The river would not be safe, either.

As Metaha looked to the distance, he saw the faint outline of the hills of Katai. It was in this place that the great chief of the Honey Dancers had ridden in search of visions.

Metaha thought to himself that it was to such a place that a great warrior should go. Many deer ran through the hills there, and fishing and trapping could be done. Strong trees afforded shade from the brightness of the summer sun, and it was known that the spirits often walked there.

The journey to the hills of Katai took Metaha three nights. He slept in the time of light, hiding beneath branches of trees cut so as to shield him from the view of his enemies. When he arrived there, Metaha climbed to a high place where Katai had once sought peace. This place Topai had spoken of many times by the light of the evening stars.

Metaha first set to the task of making hooks from mesquite thorns. Metaha sat many moments beside the streams, dipping the string he held in his hands into the water. Soon something snapped at the insects Metaha had placed on the hook, and the youth had his dinner.

Raw fish were not foreign to Metaha's taste. Many times as a boy he had tasted such food. If chewed many times and swallowed, the meat furnished strength and was little tasted. Metaha sighed as he ate the fish in this manner. Smoked, fish was one of the tastiest of foods. Raw, there was no taste to it at all.

In the time that followed the dinner, Metaha walked the land, setting snares to trap rabbits in the thick briars that spread beneath the trunks of trees. Metaha was careful to build snares that would be hidden not only from the rabbits, but from searching warriors, also.

The hills of Katai brought to Metaha a time of peace, a time of rest from the eyes of his enemies. It was a time needed in many ways.

Metaha was glad of the time of peace. The peace allowed him to make arrows, gave him time to build a small shelter in the midst of cactus and briars. There was water to drink and food to eat. And in the setting of each sun Metaha saw the dye on his flesh flake and fade. Soon his skin would be as before, and he would find himself free to begin his quest.

It was as the dye grew faint that Metaha heard the hooves of a horse nearby. He took his bow and crawled into the underbrush, searching with keen eyes for the enemy who had come upon his camp.

Metaha finally saw what he searched for, and his heart jumped at the sight. It was a single rider, a tall man wearing war paint. His chest was bare and painted in the sign of the horse spirit of the Comanches. His face was marked with the sign of the eagle. This was a man sent to kill.

Metaha had been nervous in the presence of Boltah and the Honey Dancer warriors when he caught sight of them from the shelter of his cave. This man was another thing altogether. This Comanche was not simply a searcher to be hidden from. Here was an enemy of his people, a Comanche riding into the most sacred of the lands of the Honey Dancers. Here was a man painted for war, a man armed and ready to kill.

Metaha looked deeply into the eyes of the man. He was a warrior in his prime, a man who had seen perhaps twenty summers. Metaha's eyes next fell upon a belt from which hung many scalps. Some were light hair like his own. This was a warrior who had fought the white man. This was a warrior who had killed men, not just deer and buffalo.

The warrior's body was hard and full of muscles. Even the man's legs were solid. They had the look of big trees, rough and strong. When Metaha looked back into the man's eyes, he began to understand. Here was a man with power, with the will to kill. Here was a man who could take the life of a boy without a shadow of regret.

Metaha slipped away from the man into the shelter of the trees. There he waited for the horse's hooves to die away in the distance, but this they did not do. Instead the sounds of the horse grew louder. Metaha now knew that the Comanche was on his trail.

"To each man comes the moment when he must strike out or be struck," Metaha remembered his father telling him. "It is always with a heavy heart that a man with the true spirit strikes his fellow creatures. To kill the fleet deer or the mighty buffalo is a thing that is done because there is need of food for the belly and skins to clothe the body.

"But when a man rides out into the valley in search of other men to kill, the spirit finds only shadows to cast across the life of such a man. To kill a man is a very grave thing, my son. Take the life of another man only if it must be, only if such a death shields our people from the angry eyes of an enemy."

Metaha knew the meaning of such words. It was not within his heart to kill another man. Hatred had never been a thing he understood. Not even the panther that had been killed had been struck down with an angry heart. Now this man had come to bring his death. It was to be that one of them would die.

"Spirits of the sky," Metaha said in a soft voice. "You bring to me great challenges. You know my heart has been strong when it has been made to face danger. But a chief must be more than strong in time of danger. He must do more than risk his life in battle. He must kill his enemy in time of war. This I must now do.

"I do not seek the life of this man in anger. I read the paint upon his face and hold my bow ready. If it is to be your will, let me walk away from this challenge. If it is my death you seek, I hurry to my time."

Metaha then took his bow in his hands and prepared a place to fight. This was no deer coming to drink at a pond. This was an enemy who tracked Metaha's footsteps. This was a warrior who had taken life before. This was the deadliest of game.

Metaha found a small cliff and put it to his back. Such a place would shield his back from the sharp points of arrows. Metaha waited, knowing the Comanche might appear at any moment. Metaha's arrows stood ready, and the youth concentrated on the sounds in the woods.

Soon all grew quiet, and Metaha heard the horse trotting on the hard rock of the path. He notched an arrow and prepared his shot. Then Metaha spied the horse. As he readied his fingers to let loose the arrow, Metaha was startled to see the horse had no rider. In the second he realized his enemy was elsewhere, something warned him of danger.

It is said by some that the greatest of the sky spirits reached out at that moment to warn his son. It is said by others that it was only a sudden gust of wind. Whatever it was, Metaha dove to the ground as a Comanche arrow flew through the air, shattering the stillness. The arrow landed in the side of a tree beside his head, and Metaha swallowed deeply.

Metaha had no time for thinking then. The Comanche screamed into the sky. His words filled the air with terror, and his rapid footsteps shook the earth. Metaha had but a second to turn and face the enemy.

The youth held terror in his heart. For a moment there was fear about his face. The Comanche's grim face was not twenty steps away, and the man was armed with a long war lance from which dangled three scalps and two eagle feathers. Metaha breathed in deeply, then swung his bow in the direction of the

Comanche.

Metaha held his aim, waiting for the final instant to release his arrow. The Comanche saw the youth at last, the grim frown upon his face changing to a look of great surprise.

The earth stood still for a moment. The Comanche who had had it in his heart to kill the youth held fear in his eyes; the youth stood prepared to kill his enemy. Then the Comanche screamed out a final time, and Metaha let fly the arrow.

The arrow flew true to its aim. It struck the Comanche in the chest, driving its point through the man's insides. The Comanche staggered a moment, then fell gasping to the ground. Blood squirted from the warrior's mouth, and death soon covered his face.

Metaha walked to where the man's body lay. Blood still oozed out of the wound in the man's chest, and Metaha felt no glory in his victory. Kneeling beside the dead man, Metaha looked up into the sky.

"Great spirits of the sky," Metaha cried out. "You have granted me my life, but I have purchased it at the expense of this man. It is a high price to pay for a life. Let my days be such that it will prove a bargain well made."

Metaha then took out his knife and touched it to the Comanche's forehead.

"It is our way to take a man's scalp," Metaha said to the dead man. "You bear many on your belt. I take yours with no gladness, for there is little glory in the killing of a man, even one with angry eyes."

Metaha then drove his knife under the man's scalp and cut away the thin strip of hair from the man's head. He looked over the man, taking a knife, mocassins, a jacket with much fine beadwork, even the lance the man would have used to take Metaha's life.

The youth took the Comanche's clothing and buried it under a rock. Most of it was of little use to him. He remembered riding out on the buffalo hunt once, though, when his people had discovered a young Honey Dancer killed by Comanches. The boy had been stripped and mutilated. Metaha had no wish to cut up the dead, but he wanted to make it known that Comanches were not welcome in the hills of Katai.

Metaha took the Comanche's bow and broke it against the side of a tree. The arrows were also broken. Then Metaha walked to where the Comanche's horse was grazing and looked it over.

It was a horse fit for a warrior. It had a proud head, and its legs were strong, trained to run fast in the way a warrior rides. It was sleek and well-fed, and an urge filled Metaha to throw his leg over its side and ride out across the plains. But this was not the time to be a horseman.

Metaha knelt beside the body of the dead warrior and looked up into the heavens. He watched the clouds smother the last golden glow of the sun, and he felt a coldness come over him.

"Spirits of the sky, watch over me," Metaha said. "Life holds great danger. This very morning the man here at my side rode out as a proud warrior upon a great horse. Now he lies here dead, slain by one who has not yet come to be called a man. Guard my spirit, spirits of the sky, that I might grow to know the suns of many summers."

Metaha led the horse to a small thicket and tied it to a tree. Then the youth made his way back to the shelter and prepared for sleep. It should have been a time for much shouting, a time to be feasted by his father. But that would not be. As sleep captured his thoughts, Metaha felt a cloud of danger approaching him.

XVI

The hills of Katai were not the refuge Metaha had expected. The Comanche warrior had proved that. But Metaha was no longer a boy who ran naked through the fires of his father. He was now mostly a man. He had hunted game and killed great beasts. He had faced his enemies, and when the moment had arrived to test his bow arm against the Comanche warrior, Metaha's spirit had proved its power.

Now Metaha had a horse. A warrior of the Honey Dancers riding across the buffalo valleys on the back of a horse was a sight that struck terror in the hearts of enemies and swelled the chests of friends with pride. Metaha felt as he rode out of the hills that morning that he was such a warrior, a horseman of great courage, a skilled hunter.

In the beginning of Metaha's ride he thought of nothing. The wind blew against his bare chest, reminding him of the times in the past when he had ridden beside his father to the buffalo hunts. But in those times he had ridden as a boy, and that was a thing never to be done again.

In the suns since the beginning of the ordeal of manhood, Metaha had not spent a night without the fear of being discovered by those who would bring his death. This day such fear was cast aside. Metaha left his safety in the hands of the spirits of the sky and rode across the valley in search of adventure.

Metaha had heard many times the stories of the old warriors. Often he had heard his father say that there were two ways for a warrior to flee from powerful enemies. The one was to ride in the shadows of the light, ever watchful for signs of danger. The other was to ride boldly through the open lands, acting in the way most unlikely. No enemy would foresee such action.

Metaha had tried the first way. He had hidden in the places unseen by men. He had kept no fire, slept in shelters and caves. Now he was the boldest of all, riding the Comanche horse across the broad stretches of flat land where the buffalo thundered in their great herds.

Metaha's mind filled with the stories of other warriors in other times. He had never heard of a youth killing a buffalo during the time of his ordeal. It was a thing that brightened Metaha's thoughts as he considered it. It was a thing that the youth determined to do. It was a thing that would test his courage, prove his heart to be strong in the way a chief's heart must be.

The sun crossed the skies twice without Metaha finding any signs of buffalo. Twice he watched the bright moon smile to him from the blackness of the heavens. Twice his camp stood bare among the prairie grasses, the only sign that man had ever walked the land.

On the third morning Metaha spotted the fresh trail of many buffalo. His horse seemed to sense the nearness, and Metaha found himself galloping through the high grasses. Hunger began gnawing at his stomach, and the bow stood ready. It was a ride of great distance, though, before the herd came at last into Metaha's sight.

No buffalo herd was ever startled by a single warrior. Metaha approached closely, watching the great beasts grazing in their silent way. He halted his horse when but an arrow's flight away from a great bull. Then he looked into the heavens and held out his hands.

"I do not know your face, spirit of the great buffalo," Metaha said. "I have prayed to you before on the high ground sacred to the spirits of the sky. I have stood beside my father and prayed for our people, for the food given by your children. I now ask only for the test that you might send my way. I ask only that you fill my heart with the strength to stand this challenge. It is my wish to stand tall as my father, to be a great chief of our people. If this is not to be, then I would ask a swift and brave death."

Metaha listened as the wind raced across the prairie. The buffalo herd stirred, and a great black beast stomped its way toward Metaha. It was a huge bull, and its eyes were filled with anger. Metaha's horse moved away, but the youth stilled the horse with his hand on the bridle rope. Then Metaha held the horse still by firmly pressing his legs against the horse's flanks. When he saw the buffalo pause, Metaha took out his bow and notched an arrow. Then with a shout Metaha pressed the horse forward toward the beast.

The buffalo seemed surprised by this movement. It seemed confused. The opportunity to strike was there, and Metaha drove an arrow into the shoulder of the bull as he raced past.

The buffalo turned to face the youth. Its nose snorted angrily, and it lowered its head. Then it rushed at Metaha's horse.

Metaha drew back his bowstring a second time. He was glad of the power that had come from the deer. The bowstring was taut and soon another arrow plunged into the bull's breast. The creature staggered a moment, then fell to the ground. Blood ran from its mouth, but death was not yet in its eyes. Metaha wished he had a killing lance. If the Comanche's war lance had not been left behind, the death of the bull would have come swiftly. But there was no lance, so Metaha notched another arrow.

The bull lay on the ground breathing heavily. Metaha let fly his third arrow, and the beast shuddered. Then its head hit the hard ground, and the buffalo moved no longer.

Metaha rode to the side of the animal. Its chest was covered with blood, and the ground was stained red. Metaha looked into the sky and thanked the buffalo spirit. Then he climbed down from the horse and stood beside the dead beast.

As Metaha prepared to make the throat cut, he heard the hooves of horses. He took his bow from his horse and prepared to meet whatever enemy approached. As the horsemen rode over a slight rise of ground, Metaha stared at them. He had never seen any men quite like these.

The pattern of the paint on their chests and faces

was foreign to him. He did not recognize the way they wore their hair, but he remembered his father telling of such men. These were Kiowas. They were far south of their hunting grounds.

Metaha knew the Kiowas were allies of the Comanches. He remembered the Comanche scalp he had taken but a few mornings before. But hair did not speak, and there was no way of knowing what tribe had given up such a trophy. The horse was another thing. These men might know the horse.

Metaha stood stiff as the Kiowas approached. He thought for the first time in many summers of his bright hair, of his light skin. But the Kiowas didn't seem interested. Their eyes were fixed on the buffalo that lay at Metaha's feet.

Metaha said nothing as they rode closer. He did not know if the Kiowas spoke the same language as the Honey Dancers. He did not know if the Kiowas knew about the white dye. If they did not, Metaha might have a chance. If they did, he would soon be dead.

One of the Kiowas rode out from the others. He was a small man dressed in a deerskin vest with bright blue paint stripes. His chest was bare, and Metaha could tell the power that rested in his great bulging arms. The Kiowa warrior rode close to the buffalo and looked down on Metaha. Then the man screamed out loudly, and the others joined him. When the screaming finally stopped, the Kiowas rode off after the buffalo herd, leaving Metaha alone on the prairie.

The Kiowas chased the herd away toward the sun, and Metaha started the difficult task of skinning the beast and readying the meat. It was strange that he hadn't seemed afraid of the Kiowas. Even now, as he tended the buffalo carcass, he had no fear of Boltah or the other warriors coming to strike him down.

The sun was nearly down when Metaha finished with the beast. He rolled the hide onto the back of his horse and cut strips of meat to be smoked. He then took the great horns from the buffalo and cut out its tongue and heart to be dedicated to the buffalo spirit. Then Metaha climbed onto the back of his horse and rode away.

Metaha rode into the darkness, crossing small hills, passing stands of mesquite trees, weaving his way across the valleys in the direction of the hills of Katai. He finally came to a stream. It was in this place that he made his camp.

Metaha was tired from the long ride. His skin was covered with the blood of the buffalo, and there was a smell of death about him. He tied the horse to a small shrub and walked to the stream. There he washed the blood and sweat from his skin, making him feel partly human again. Then he looked up into the heavens at the sparkling stars overhead.

"Spirits of the sky, you have brought me great honor," Metaha spoke softly. "Give me the strength to complete my ordeal. Give power to my feet that they may lead me home to my people. Most of all grant me wisdom to do what I am to do. Show me the light that I might follow it. Guard me from the shadows when they hold danger."

When Metaha had spoken the last of these words, he lay down and closed his eyes. Sleep soon took possession of his weary body, but it was not a sleep filled with peace.

The dream came upon him suddenly. He saw a

bright light which seemed to blind him. A great golden glow filled the dream. In the midst of this glow a rocky mountain flooded the dream. Metaha felt pain as the mountain appeared. His feet were torn by jagged rocks. His hands bled as they struggled to get a grip on the rugged mountainside.

The mountain was no easy thing to be climbed. Metaha watched as the vision grew clearer. He could see himself standing tall against a clear sky. He could see a look of triumph on his face. Then the dream echoed with the sound of thunder, and the mountain vanished.

Next Metaha found himself standing naked before a wide river. The waters lapped at Metaha's feet, and he saw himself searching for a place to cross. Then a great wind swept him up into the air, and it was as if he walked across the waters.

There was a feeling of power within Metaha. He saw himself changed into an eagle. The bird flew high above the river and soared in a great circle. Then Metaha became a man again.

The dream lost its golden glow as Metaha saw himself disappear. The great river was gone also. All that was left was a haunting darkness. In the midst of this darkness came a terrible cry, a hideous scream that shook him even in his sleep.

From out of the darkness Metaha could see nothing. Then two terrible green eyes peered at him. As Metaha's eyes filled with the sight of the green eyes, great white teeth bared themselves, flashing in the moonlight. A deep growl was heard, and Metaha felt pain rip through him. The white teeth grew red, then vanished. It was at this moment that Metaha saw himself standing tall against the clear sky a second time.

Once again the dream was flooded with golden light. A huge eagle crossed the sky, circling over Metaha's head. The eagle swooped lower each of the three times it circled the sky. The dream flashed red, and there was a terrible cry from the eagle. An arrow flew through the air and drove itself into the heart of the bird. Then the skies filled with lightning, and there was a smell of death in the air.

The dream ended at that moment. There was no gentle voice speaking to him. No feeling of freedom filled his heart as it had when he had turned into the eagle to fly above the river. No soft wind cooled the warmth of the summer air. Only the smell of death lingered.

On another night Metaha might have stirred from his sleep. Another time he might have sought to discover the message the spirits had sent him. But this was a night after a day that had left the youth weary, and sleep was not a thing to be given away.

When morning came, Metaha walked back to the stream. He tended the horse, seeing that its feet were sound, that its head was cool in the way a horse should be at sunrise. Metaha found the horse strong and cool. A Comanche lives and dies as his horse does, and the warrior who had owned this animal had meant to live long.

As the sunlight broke over his camp, Metaha made his way into the stream. Its cooling waters brought new life to him, and he dipped his head into the stream so that water dribbled across his forehead. As he felt the water drain from his hair, he realized he had been away from the village of his father for many suns.

"The time to complete my ordeal nears," he whispered to the wind as he looked at his image in the water. Gone was the white dye. Gone was the look of a boy he had carried with him into the wilderness.

His hair had grown back, and there was the power of every Honey Dancer from the time of Katai in his bow arm, in his solid shoulders, in his fleet feet and firm belly.

"My time nears, spirits of the sky," Metaha spoke. "I am now to find the meaning of the dream. I must climb the tall mountain, cross the great river. I must battle the creature of the night, even though it will taste my blood. And then I will set forth on the greatest quest."

As Metaha spoke those last words, the wind howled in a strange way, and a dark cloud swallowed the sun. The eagle in the dream was remembered. There was a warning there. But its meaning was lost. No voice spoke to Metaha, no wise words came from his father or from the sky to tell him of the danger that sought him. But Metaha had faced dangers, and it would be but another to be faced.

There was first of all the mountain, and that was enough of a challenge that morning.

XVII

To climb a mountain is never a small thing. Metaha remembered the dream, remembered the feeling of pain that had filled his heart as the flesh was torn from his hands and feet. But he remembered also that it had been a thing that had been done. So it was that he set off to the hills of Katai with courage and confidence flooding his mind.

Metaha rode swiftly across the broad flatlands of the buffalo valley. The Comanche horse bore him as truly as the wind bore the eagle. The sun was dying in the hills when Metaha finally saw the mountain. It was a great jagged pile of rock. There was no hint of gentle slope to this place. No trees covered its sides. It was a place full of danger.

There were many other mountains to be found near the place where Metaha stood. Most of the high places known to the Honey Dancers were to be found in the hills of Katai, but there was no other mountain so difficult to climb. But it was, after all was considered, the place Metaha had seen in his dream.

"I see and understand," Metaha spoke, looking

into the heavens. "It is to be the greatest of challenges for me, spirits of the sky. It is to be no small thing for me to set my feet upon the top of such a mountain."

The wind blew across the land, sweeping back the hair from Metaha's forehead. It was his answer. Knowing it was the thing to be done, Metaha took from the horse his belongings and cast a sorrowful look at the animal.

"You have borne me safely across the buffalo valleys," Metaha said. "You have brought me to the place of my trials bravely. I now send you upon your way."

Saying what he felt in his heart, Metaha waved a buffalo hide at the horse, and the animal flew away from him. It ran until Metaha's eyes could find no sign of it. Metaha felt empty without the horse at his side, but if his enemies caught sight of the horse there, it would be but a simple thing to hunt the mountain for Metaha. His death would surely follow.

There was little need of a horse now. Metaha was beginning his quest, and each thing was to be taken in turn. No part of the quest brought the need for a horse.

Metaha cut from a small tree several vines and bound to his naked back all of his possessions. There was the buffalo hide, the horns, much dried meat, and his bow and arrows. He knew such weight would hinder his climb, but there would be little chance of coming back for it. Each thing was important. What was not was left behind.

When the tying was completed, Metaha took the moccasins he had made and tied them together. These he placed around his neck. Climbing with bare feet was a thing full of pain, but toes were better suited to clawing away at the earth than moccasins.

In the beginning the mountain posed no. great hardships. But as darkness swallowed the sun, Metaha found the going difficult. There were few trees to aid his weary legs. When he came to a small cave, he decided to pause for the brightness the sun would bring.

The night was filled with many sounds, and little rest came to Metaha. Birds scurried outside the cave, bringing food to their nests in the high cracks that scarred the mountain. His ears were filled many times with the sounds of rattlesnakes. There was the howl of the wolf, the cry of the panther. The night air was alive with danger, and every minute Metaha gripped his bow tighter.

When a panther stalked the ground beside the cave, Metaha grew worried. Then he remembered the dream. The terrible eyes and bloody teeth of the night creature followed Metaha's climb to the top of the mountain. There was no danger to be faced on the mountain. And so it was that sleep filled his weary body.

He awoke as the sun bathed the hills in its golden glow. It was as if the spirits of the sky had poured a golden bowl of water on the land. Everything was brilliant, and Metaha felt his heart stir. It was on such a day that a young man should meet the first of his challenges.

Soon Metaha's feet clawed away at the mountainside. Step after step was taken. More and more of the mountain came to be below him. But the more he climbed, the more he saw lay ahead of him still.

The ground grew steeper. Metaha had to search with his fingers for small crevices to serve as toeholds. He found himself straining every muscle to lift his slight frame over the rocky cliffside. Sharp rocks tore into the bare skin of his thighs; rock ripped the flesh from his back and sides. His soft cheeks were pressed close to the hard mountain, and tears of agony mixed with blood as they wove their way down his face and onto his chest.

There was nothing glorious about this struggle. It was a thing filled only with pain. But the mastering of this mountain would make his heart strong, and as he cried to the sky spirits for help, he thanked them for the strength to go on. And on he did go. As he took every step, he wondered that he was not standing upon the highest place of the mountain. But there was always another cliff, always another great crack in the mountain to be crossed.

"Spirits of the sky!" Metaha cried out. "Why do you taunt me? You grow this mountain taller for every step I take."

But the wind did not answer, and Metaha was ashamed for blaming the spirits for his own lack of strength. Even if the mountain were to grow a hundred times, he told himself, I will still see myself standing upon the high ground, looking to the valleys below me.

It was then that he reached the cliff of eagles. He had heard of this place from his father. Other warriors had come here to collect the feathers of eagles to place them in war bonnets. These bonnets were precious to the Honey Dancers above all others, and Metaha remembered dreaming of this place as a boy.

158

Many boys left the lodges of their fathers to ride to the cliff of eagles, but none ever climbed the mountain to reach the place. Metaha looked around him at the discarded feathers of many birds. There were enough there to make a great war bonnet. For a moment Metaha thought to collect them. Then he remembered his quest was to seek the feather of the owl. It would not be right for a youth to bring to his people a great war bonnet. Such a thing was for a medicine chief or a warrior who had killed many enemies of his people.

To Metaha the cliff of eagles now brought a great danger. He could look above and see the great birds hovering over their nests. Metaha looked to see if there was a way to the top of the mountain around this cliff, but there was no such place. To climb meant to come close by the nests of eagles.

Metaha remembered a nightmare he had had as a boy. There was a warrior among the Honey Dancers, a man named Kaquatamas. The name meant eagle eye, but it had not been a name won by keen sight.

Kaquatamas had went once in his youth to the cliff of eagles, determined to scale the rugged cliff. As he climbed, a great eagle had soared across the sky, blocking out the sun. Kaquatamas had turned his head and stared in terror as the great claws of the eagle reached down and sank into the tender flesh of his shoulder. Kaquatamas had screamed into the air, shaking the eagle away.

Kaquatamas had been filled with fear and pain. As he tried to make his way down the side of the cliff, the eagle had swept down and torn a great gash in the side of his face. Kaquatamas was robbed of an eye, and the boy had tumbled from the cliff, breaking a leg in such a way that he was lame forever.

Metaha remembered Kaquatamas. He had been an old man in the first summer of Metaha's life. Kaquatamas never rode to battle, for he was crippled. But it was said that when the eagle robbed him of his eye, a great medicine power had come to the man. Kaquatamas saw things that were to come, and he was honored among the medicine chiefs of his people.

Metaha thought to himself that it was the way of the spirits to give gifts to a man who had lost much. Other warriors who had suffered great losses had also been given strange powers. But Metaha was young, and he did not wish a life of half-blindness, a life of limping through the summers of his old age.

Metaha looked up at the nests of the eagles. He breathed deeply. It was the way his father had taught him. Such breathing often kept away the grip of fear. Metaha had need of such breathing that moment.

"Great and powerful eagles," Metaha said, swallowing. "Great and most mighty of all birds, hear my words! They are but spoken by a small voice in a place filled with many great voices, the voices of the wind and sky. I do not walk among you to bring you harm. I would be as a whisper as I step among the places dear to your hearts. I come now, sent by the spirits of the sky, that I might stand on the high ground and feel a closeness to the heavens."

Metaha felt a rush of wind against his shoulders, and the wings of an eagle stirred the quiet of the day.

"Spirits of the sky," Metaha whispered, "I come now to meet what will come to be my fate."

As the wind died away, Metaha started his climb. His eyes were fixed on the nests of the eagles. Three times the great birds flew close beside him, but he did not cry out. A peace settled over him, and he knew he had nothing to fear from the birds. It was like the time Boltah had left him in the place of the snakes.

The cliff was not a place easily scaled, and Metaha cast from his mind the eagles so that he could concentrate on the task of climbing. His hands and feet scratched away at the rocky cliff, and bit by bit he climbed. When he was at last able to pull himself up to the ledge of the eagle nests, he did not linger. He walked softly away from the nests, careful not to step upon the bones of the dead, careful not to stir the many feathers that lay in that place. As Metaha departed the cliff of the eagles, he sang in his heart a song of thanks to the spirits of the sky.

With the cliff of the eagles behind him, the going became easier. But soon Metaha came upon another great obstacle to his quest. There was a great chasm, a wide gap that could not be crossed by a man without a rope. Metaha cast his eyes down, then noticed beneath him a tree. Beside this tree grew a strong vine of a type his father had spoken of. This vine could be woven into a rope of great strength, and Metaha set to doing that very thing. He set aside his possessions and wove the rope. As the sky grew black, Metaha had made a rope of great strength and length.

The crossing of the chasm would be a thing best left to the light of morning, so Metaha gathered leaves and made a soft bed. He lay back upon the leaves and found a restful sleep.

Morning found Metaha refreshed from his difficult climb of the cliff of eagles. He felt the power in his arms, then picked up the rope he had made. He took the rope in his hands and threw it across the chasm so that the loop in the far end fell upon the stump of a tree and held fast. Metaha then tied the loose end to a strong tree and prepared to cross.

In his few summers of life Metaha had been in danger many times. But as he tied his possessions to his back, he knew he had rarely faced a more certain death. If the rope was weak or his hands slipped, he would find himself smashed against the rocks at the base of the mountain far below.

Metaha had prayed to the sky spirits many times to deliver him from danger. This danger he knew must be faced alone. It was a test of his own strength, a test to be met by himself.

Metaha took the rope firmly in his hands and threw his feet together over the vine in such a way that his body balanced on the single strand of rope. Then he began the crossing, feeling the rope sag as his body loosened the rope's ends. Metaha's eyes watched the earth far below.

He felt as an eagle must have felt upon its first flight. He trembled as he imagined his youthful body lying below, its bones shattered, the hand of death upon his face. He dreaded the vision of his eyes filled with the darkness of death.

The sun stood high in the heavens when Metaha finally neared the far side of the chasm. Looking back, he could see the broken strands of rope behind him. He could only hope the power in his hands would not fail him. He could only pray that the rope he had made would be strong enough to support him for the time it took to complete the crossing.

More strands broke in the passing of each moment.

Metaha's heart jumped as the rope grew weaker. Now he was near the far edge, and his legs pushed him onward. He would not allow himself to die when living was so close.

Then the rope snapped. Metaha did not know if the other end had given way or if some fiber in the center had at last yielded to the strain. He only felt himself flung downward. His arms were strong, though, and he held his grip. His hands were torn and bloodied by the rope, but they still held on. His bare knees were rubbed raw against the rope. His shoulder was slammed against the face of the cliff. Looking up, he saw that he was but the height of three men from the edge of the cliff above him, and that what rope remained seemed strong.

Metaha swallowed the pain and cried out in the silent air to his father. Then he began climbing. If the cliff of eagles had brought pain, this cliff brought agony. His hands were torn so that he could see the bare muscles and bones of his fingers. Blood ran across his arms so that he could smell it. His head grew light, and his eyes did not see in the clear way they had before. He found himself dreaming, but it was not a time to dream. He struggled on, reaching out for the cliff that would bring safety.

Metaha's head filled with a thousand memories. He found himself running through the fires of old warriors, swimming naked in the river as a boy. He remembered how soft the touch of his mother had been, how wonderful the summer flowers had smelled when he brought them for her. He remembered the soft words of his father, the leathery touch of the old chief's hands. He remembered the smiles of Topai.

But most of all he remembered the laughing face of Boltah as the old priest had left him among the snakes.

"Evil one," Metaha whispered, blinking away the tears of pain that clouded his eyes. "I will stand before the council of my father and bring him honor. I am not one to die on this mountain."

It was with new power grown from a sense of duty, of pride, of hatred, that Metaha pulled himself across the edge of the chasm and looked below to the place where his shattered body might have lain.

"I was not brought so far to lie there," he said quietly.

Then he walked on, binding his raw hands as he went.

XVIII

There was enough of the boy left in Metaha to bring a smile to his lips when he stood at last upon the summit of the mountain. It was a moment he would not soon forget. The warm summer breeze blew furiously across his face, stinging his eyes so that he could keep them open only with great effort. The sun was brilliant, casting the same golden glow across the land it had that morning.

It is strange, Metaha thought to himself, that so much could have been made to fill a single day. He wondered if the sun had known that morning what ordeals would fill the moments of that single journey across the heavens. Perhaps, he thought, that was the reason for such a brilliant glow.

Metaha stepped to an outcropping of rock and looked far below at the valley. Then he looked up into the sky.

"Spirits of the sky, you sent to me a dream to give me strength. You showed me this mountain could be tamed. All I have done is to bring honor to you and my father. All I have done you have written so that my heart would grow strong."

Metaha cast his eyes away from the clear sky and looked again to the valley.

"Mountain, I have set my feet upon your back!" Metaha called out boldly. "I have mastered the cliffs and chasms you have set before me. I have felt the bite of your rocks, have known the peril you have brought to me. Still, I stand upon you, warrior that I will become Your spirit now belongs to me, mountain. Let it lead me to greatness. Let it remind me that life and death are things closely linked, and that only the power the spirits have sent to fill my arms, my shoulders, my heart, have carried me to this place."

Metaha listened as the wind stirred, blowing with such fury that his deerskin vest was swept away from his shoulders.

"May I prove worthy of this moment," Metaha said, searching the valley again. "Watch over me in my trials, mountain spirit, and give me the strength you have set against me this day."

Metaha now stepped away from the outcropping and looked below with great care. At last he caught sight of what he searched for. A great line of blue cut its way between two small mountains not far from where he stood. He remembered the words of Boltah. His second task was to set his bare feet upon the great waters.

"How is this to be done?" Metaha called out to the sky spirits. "In the dream I flew across as an eagle. But I have no wings to carry me. No man can walk upon the waters."

The wind whined, creating an unearthly sound. Metaha was shaken, and he stepped back beside a tall tree that grew upon the mountaintop. Darkness would soon be upon the land, so Metaha chose to make his camp there for the night.

A great hunger seized him, and he tore into the dried meat as a hungry wolf might. He ate much, feeling the power return to his bones. He tended to his torn flesh, washing the wounds with clear water taken from a mountain spring. Metaha slept well that night, untroubled by the panther or the wolf that crept beside his feet. It was as if his life was protected by the spirits of the sky, and no harm could come to him from beast or man.

As the first rays of sunlight brightened the mountain that next morning, Metaha sprang to his feet. The meat and spring water had done their work well. He was refreshed and eager to proceed with his quest. Three days had been devoted to the mountain, and there must be no time lost in completing his quest.

Metaha bound his torn feet and put on his moccasins. Then he set out down the mountain, bound for the river. The going was little easier than before, but Metaha felt stronger. His hands and feet seemed molded to the rocks. It was as if the mountain had surrendered. Metaha truly owned its spirit, and the rocks and youth were as one.

It was near nightfall when Metaha reached the river. It was a branch of the great giver of life that flowed through the camps of the Honey Dancers, and Metaha paused to sing a song his mother had always loved.

"Great waters, take my song to her," Metaha said. "My heart longs for her gentle words, and hers is sick in my absence. May these words warm her, give her new life."

It comforted Metaha to know the waters at his feet would soon wash against the places dear to his heart. But he wasted little time on such thoughts. There was the river to be faced.

"Boltah, you set me no small task," Metaha said under his breath, "to walk with bare feet upon the great waters. This is a puzzle indeed."

Metaha walked along the side of the river. He tested the depth of the water. It was said that often the waters grew shallow in places where horses could cross without getting their flanks wet. There was no such place Metaha could find, and he knew the rivers of the hills of Katai well.

Metaha sat down upon a rock and pondered the problem. It was a thing that was done in the dream, yet he could not see how. He was a man, not an eagle. He could grow no feathers and fly upon the wind. Then he heard a great cry from the river, and his eyes beheld a strange sight. A great eagle was standing in the midst of the waters, flapping its great wings and crying out to the heavens.

For a moment Metaha could not understand what was happening. He did not know how an eagle could stand upon the waters. Then the eagle flew away, and Metaha saw the eagle had stood upon a branch of a tall tree swept along the waters.

"Great eagle, even now you must guide me upon my quest," Metaha cried out. "Even now you feel pity for the foolish one who is shown all, but who cannot see with the true light of the sky spirits. When morning comes, I will stand upon the great waters in my bare feet."

The night brought a strangeness with it. The stars were brighter than before, and Metaha could not close his eyes on them. They sparkled above, flashing words to him alone. He could hear the wind singing through the trees, and he knew the sky spirits were speaking about him.

When morning came, Metaha busied himself hacking limbs from trees so that he could bind them together. He fashioned first a wooden framework, then covered it with branches woven together to make a strong mat. It was the way shelters were made by the mountain people. It made a strong platform, strong enough to support the weight of the youth and his possessions.

Metaha next shaped a large smooth piece of wood. This he placed on the back of the platform. It was a thing the Honey Dancers had learned before the time of Katai. Such a smooth piece of wood was always attached to canoes. The river rarely swallowed such a canoe, and strong warriors could then go where they would upon the wings of the river.

"This will be my wings," Metaha said. "I will fly on the waters, touching their mighty spirit with my bare feet. Just as the mountain and I are one, so it will be with the great giver of all life."

Metaha took his small craft and tied his possessions firmly to it. Then he took it to the river and set it in the waters. The river pulled at the craft, almost sweeping it away before Metaha could stand upon it. When Metaha finally stood on the platform, the river swept both away as an eagle might sweep away a small rabbit.

Metaha's knees buckled at first, and it was all he

could do to steady himself. The waters covered the craft, and the youth looked down to see his bare feet upon the waters. If the spirits of the sky had looked down at that moment, Metaha knew it must have seemed to them that here was a youth who could walk upon the waters of the earth.

Metaha's journey upon the waters was as no thing he had done before. The waters held him as a small boy holds a cricket. The cricket squirms and tries to find freedom, but the boy holds tightly. Metaha felt as if a hand had reached down from the sky to shape his course. He looked to the far side of the river, hoping the waters would sweep him there. But whenever the craft approached, the strong current of the river would pull it back away.

Metaha felt at first as he had in the dream. His spirit soared. It was as if he was above his body, flying through the air beside the eagle. It was as if he could see all, as if his spirit belonged to the heavens.

But as the craft was swept on by the river, the youth faltered. His legs grew weak, and his head grew light. His eyes no longer saw clearly, and he grew weary of the journey. As if possessed by something foreign, something not understood, Metaha acted strangely. His feet began moving, and as they moved the craft was guided.

For many moments the craft did little. Then it steadily grew closer to the far side of the great giver of life. Metaha could no longer see the mountains where he had first stood beside the river. He was now far from the place where he had cut the branches. Soon he would be in the place where his quest must end.

The craft began to slow as the grasp of the river

spirits lessened. Soon Metaha felt himself break away from the current and glide into a backwater. He stood still as the craft floated to the far side of the river. Then he untied his possessions and stepped onto the land.

His legs were weary, and he stumbled. After standing upon the waters, it seemed strange to Metaha that he should fall when once again standing upon the firm earth.

"It is your way, spirits of the sky, to remind a man that he is but a man," Metaha said solemnly. "A man is never so great as his eyes would make him I now seek the completion of my quest, spirits. Walk with me through this time of danger, for I know from the dream that it is now that I have most to fear of all."

Metaha took out the dried meat and ate. His legs were still weak, and they would not support him. It would be best to stay beside the river where there would be water and food. He would seek the last tasks when the sun brought morning.

Metaha washed himself as the sun died in the mountains. He cast away the dirt and sweat of a hard day. Then he bathed his raw hands and feet in an ointment made from the roots of river plants. When he was rested and well-fed, he took to a soft bed of leaves and water lilies.

He found for the first time in many days a peace he had never known away from the lodge of his father. It was a peace longed for, a peace he thought he had lost forever. It was a peace that would make his spirit strong like the mountain, powerful like the river. It was a thing needed most by a youth who would return to his village as a warrior.

XIX

The peace that had filled Metaha's sleep did not last. Something moved in the brush beside his camp, and the youth sprang to his feet. The nights of terror when Metaha had lain awake in fear of a hundred enemies came back to him. As his eyes searched the brush for some sign of an intruder, he clothed himself and notched an arrow in his bowstring.

No sound came from the brush. Metaha wiped the sweat away from his forehead and relaxed. Perhaps it was all in a dream, Metaha thought to himself. But then the sound returned, and he remembered the quest.

"You must fight a creature of the night," Boltah had told him.

"So, you have come to test my courage," Metaha said, a smile coming to his lips. "What are you, panther or wolf, man or spirit?"

As Metaha spoke, a low growl came from the woods. The sound brought a shudder to Metaha's spine, and he looked in that direction.

"So you are a beast," Metaha said. "Beasts have

cast their eyes upon me before. I have killed them even as I will kill you. Come forth, beast, and show yourself. My bow is strong, and I see with the true eyes of a warrior. I will not make you wait long for your death."

The creature grew silent. Metaha could hear its panting in the woods not far distant, but it was not the way of a Honey Dancer to challenge a creature of the night in the places known best to the beast. Wisdom told a warrior to seek battle in an open place, where an arrow might find its mark with greater ease.

Metaha had never known such uneasiness. As he waited for the creature's attack, he remembered the blood in his dream. He remembered the pain. But the thing that he could not bear was the waiting.

Many times Metaha had fought. Many times he had killed beasts stronger than himself. Many times he had stood tall upon the field of battle and done what a warrior did. But he had never before known the agony of waiting upon an enemy.

Metaha could smell the evil presence in the brush. He sensed the spirit of the other as it watched him. He remembered the dream again, remembered the terrifying green eyes of the beast. But there was nothing to be done. Waiting was all there was.

Metaha felt the sweat of his hand loosen his grip on the bow. His arm grew tired of keeping the arrow taut on his bowstring. His eyes grew heavy, and he longed for the comfort of sleep. Then he heard the stirring of the wind. The trees moved, and he faced at last the terrible green eyes.

"So you have come," Metaha said, the power returning to his bow arm. "So you have come at last to test me. You will not find me wanting. I am strong and of great courage. You who come with evil eyes to hunt me will die this night."

The growling grew louder, and Metaha knew at last his enemy. It was a wolf. From the sound of its voice it was the terrible gray wolf that hunted among the trees of the hills. It was a creature to be feared above others.

When the eyes stood still for many moments, Metaha swung his bow in their direction and fired an arrow. The arrow flew toward the eyes, but the wolf moved away in an instant, and the arrow failed to find its mark.

The wolf now charged, racing as if shot by the sky spirits themselves. The beast hit Metaha full force as the youth was notching a second arrow, and the youth lost his grip on the bow. The bow flew away one way, and Metaha rolled away in the other direction.

Metaha groaned, but he had no time for thought now. In another instant the wolf was upon him, standing on the youth's chest and sinking its teeth into the soft flesh of Metaha's side. —

Metaha screamed, then took out his knife and plunged it into the wolf's face, putting out an eye. The beast staggered back, and the blood of man and creature of the night mingled on the rocky ground.

"Now you feel the bite of my knife," Metaha said angrily. "Come and let me finish you."

The wolf growled furiously, shaking the blood from its face. The remaining green eye blazed red, and it leaped at Metaha. This time the youth was ready. Metaha blocked the vicious teeth away with his forearm and stabbed again with his knife, cutting into the

175

underbelly of the creature. The wolf howled in pain, but it ripped great tears in Metaha's bare legs. The youth fell back this time, and the wolf grabbed Metaha's right wrist in its jagged teeth.

"You have not beaten me, wolf," Metaha cried, kicking the beast away. "I will write your death."

Metaha stumbled toward his bow and notched an arrow. As the beast glared at him with one furious eye, Metaha fired an arrow into the beast's chest.

The wolf stopped for a minute, and Metaha thought it dead. But this was a creature filled with an evil heart, and evil things are never quick to die. The creature sprang forward again, clawing and biting at the youth. Metaha blocked the beast's attack with the bow, then tried to finish it with his knife. It was not a thing to be done, though.

So it was that the two of them lay there together for much of the night. Each was prepared to strike the fatal blow, but neither could find the opportunity. Blood was spilled, and death hung in the ear. Metaha watched the wolf's single eye grow dim as the life flowed out of its chest. He felt his own life-thread grow weak. Soon the power of his arm would be gone. The power needed to strike down the creature and insure Metaha's survival grew faint.

That was when Metaha heard a sound. It was a strange sound spoken to him in an unknown, strangely foreign voice.

"Have strength, my son," the voice said. "Strike down your enemy. I will send you the strength."

Metaha shook with fear upon hearing the voice. It was an alien voice, yet he had heard it before. Then he suddenly knew where. It was the voice heard always in his dreams. It was the sky spirits telling him to strike.

"You must die now!" Metaha screamed, his body consumed by pain. "It is now the moment for me to kill you!"

The beast seemed to understand, for the fury in its eye faded. Then it leaped at him, and Metaha's knife flashed in the moonlight. The youth cut deeply into the wolf's vitals. The creature wailed in pain, then struck the ground, rolling beside Metaha's feet.

Metaha prepared to strike the creature again, but something stopped him. The voice was still in the air, but it seemed to cry out for no more fighting. Looking at the wolf, Metaha saw that his enemy was dead. There would be no more battle that night.

Metaha felt the blood flow from the gashes in his arms and legs and side, but the pain departed. He bent over the wolf and cut off its head. Then he hurriedly skinned the beast, throwing the bloody carcass into the woods for the birds to devour.

"Spirits of the sky!" Metaha cried out. "You have given me this great victory. It is your honor that is proved. I will not fail you, spirits. I will grow to be tall and proud even as my father. You will not find me without courage or honor as I complete my quest."

A great quiet filled the place. Metaha walked slowly to the river and stripped himself. He bathed his torn flesh, allowing the life-giving waters to restore the power he had lost to the wolf. Then he chanted the medicine chants that would send away the evil odors of disease from his broken flesh. When this was done, he boiled herbs and coated his wounds with their liquids.

"Make me strong, great giver of life," Metaha

spoke to the river. "Make my bow arm strong and my heart stronger, spirits of the sky," he said, looking into the heavens. "And make my eyes see all there is to see. Let me have the wisdom of my father that I might see the good and the bad, even as he does."

It was as these last words were spoken that the earth trembled. Great flashes of lightning tore the sky, and Metaha grew fearful. The sky was alive with violence, and it was not a thing thought to spell good fortune. Evil walked the high places, and Metaha knew something far more dangerous than a wolf or a river or even a Comanche lay ahead to be faced. His mind was uneasy as he bound his wounds. Then he rested his head on the soft leaves of his bed and sought sleep.

XX

Metaha began the final part of his quest even as the sun first greeted the sky. He would have preferred to spend a day of rest beside the river, but too many days had passed since he had set out from the village, and he was eager to return.

As he walked, the wounds on his arms and legs brought great pain. The tear in his side was not deep, though, and the flesh there was barely broken. Metaha paused to cut a walking staff, which could ease the pain of walking.

Metaha did not walk far. He was in the hills of Katai already, and it was in that place where he was to battle the great horned owl. So it was that he chose the first mountain he came upon to climb and seek his vision.

It was not a difficult mountain to climb. There were no great cliffs or deep chasms to be crossed. But there was a high ledge that overlooked the buffalo valleys, and it was to this place that Metaha went.

Many times he had seen his father prepare for a vision. To stand before the sky spirits on a high place was no small thing for a man to do. Metaha had heard of men seeking such a vision who had been struck by bolts of lightning, for their hearts had been filled with evil. But Metaha knew his heart held only truth and honor, and he was not afraid.

He set down his possessions and took only the hide of the wolf. This he attached to the beast's great head, which Metaha had treated in the way he had learned from his father. The wolf's head he set upon his own so that it seemed to be half man, half creature of the night.

Metaha then made from the ground a red paste. This paste he smeared on his bare chest, his arms and thighs. Then he stripped himself so that only the wolf's hide covered his back. It was the way a man bared himself before the spirits, bared himself to show the spirits he knew he was still but a man, still but a soft creature who walked the land only because the sky spirits sent the rains, made him strong of heart, provided game to fill his belly and test his courage.

It was in this way that Metaha walked to the high place and began to chant to the spirits of the sky.

Great spirits of the sky,
A man is but dust blowing in the summer breeze.
A man is less than the sand bathed by the giver of
    all life.
A man is nothing.
It is through the truth sent by you
That we know this.
It is because our hearts are strong,
Because we have ridden to battle,
Because we have been called upon to live

That we call ourselves warriors.
All that I have is from you.
The waters that cool my soul,
That ease my thirst,
That bring the fish for me to eat
Are sent by you.
The sun that lights the sky
And warms the earth comes from you.
You send the buffalo and the deer.
You show me the true ways
When all is dark.
You shield me from those
Who would take my life.
Now I embark upon the last of my tasks.
I set out upon the spirit quest
Which will mark me as a warrior.
If I am strong, guide me
That I might become a chief of my people,
That I might make the Honey Dancers a people
Known to all.
If I am weak,
Let me not return.
I would not bring shame to my father
Or my people.
This is the song of Metaha,
The light sent from heaven
To my father, great Waseta.
Let an answer come to me in the night.

Metaha chanted in this way three times. Each time
he shouted the chant with a voice louder than before.
At last his voice could speak no longer, and he threw
off the wolf's hide and stood naked before the stars.

"Hear me, father sky," Metaha whispered. "I stand before you as I stood on the day of my birth. Send me your light that I might follow it. Warm me with your smiles that I might prosper."

The sky grew unsettled, and thunder shook the earth. Metaha listened as the wind blew against his back. He felt uneasy. It was as though something touched his shoulder. Then it was gone, and the skies were still.

"My answer must come in the night," Metaha said sadly. "I must bring the vision."

Bringing a vision was nothing easily done. The spirits of the sky spoke only as they wished, and Metaha knew their voices well. They had spoken many times to him in his trials. They had given him signs to guide him. Now they were silent and would speak again only if he showed it was a thing merited by his own sacrifice.

Metaha built a great fire. As the fire burned, he set himself close beside it in such a way that his flesh was burned by the flames.

Next Metaha took his knife and tore thin strips of his flesh from his hands and feet. He then cut his chest so that the bright blood of his youth dripped across his stomach. His head soon grew light, and a fever raged inside him.

"Speak to me, spirits of the sky," Metaha prayed, bowing his head so that his eyes could not see the blazing stars overhead. "Speak to me that I might know the light of your wisdom."

Metaha's mind grew cloudy. He could see nothing but darkness. Then he heard laughter, and he tried to see from where it came. It was a voice he had heard before, but it had no face.

"Speak to me clearly, spirits," Metaha said. "Brighten the dimness of my life from your wisdom."

Then the fever raged in the youth's forehead, and he slumped forward. He could now see nothing, feel nothing, hear nothing. All was darkness.

It remained this way for a long time. Metaha felt himself drifting through the voids of space. He had no eyes with which to see, no mouth with which to speak. His ears could not hear; his fingers could not touch.

Then the darkness opened up, and a great light shone forth. From the light came an eagle. It flew in three great circles. At Metaha's feet fell a great feather, the gift of the eagle.

But Metaha heard the laugh, and a strong arm took up a bow and sent an arrow into the body of the eagle. As the arrow pierced the heart of the eagle, Metaha felt a great pain. His chest collapsed, and he knew the darkness of night.

It was a strange thing. The eagle had been like Metaha, but the bow arm that had killed had been Metaha's, too. It was a thing not to be understood.

Metaha awoke with fever. His head was on fire, and his chest and arms were covered with blood. He found a spring and purified himself. Then he thought about the vision.

"The eagle is the sky spirit's messenger," Metaha said. "More than once the spirits have sent him to me. He has brought me the gift of an eagle feather."

Metaha paused when he thought of this. Many times he had heard boys speak of bringing an eagle feather back from their quest. Such could be understood. But Boltah had sent Metaha after the feather

183

of the great horned owl. Mataha had never seen man or woman with the feather of an owl. But Boltah had said it was a thing for a chief to do.

The youth felt clouds of confusion. There was no understanding. Meaning was in the vision, but there were many things wrong. It should have been an owl, not an eagle. That would have been clear.

Could the spirits have become confused? Metaha wondered. He could not see how such things as what he had seen would come to pass. But it was the nature of a spirit quest for some things not to be understood. So it was that Metaha accepted what had been and what was to be.

Two nights Metaha spent on the mountain. He tended his wounds and fought the fever. Each night the same message came. Each night Metaha grew more concerned.

"Beware," a voice whispered to him from the final dream.

But he did not know what it was that should be feared. Who should he beware of? What danger awaited him?

XXI

Metaha wove his way through the darkness, ever wary of the night sounds all around him. The crickets chirped, and the birds sang out their warnings that an intruder had come. Behind him Metaha heard the mournful howl of a wolf. He remembered how the sounds had terrified him as a child. Many nights he had trembled at the thought of being snatched away from his father's fire by a wolf. Such had happened before.

Now Metaha greeted each sound as an old friend. He knew each bird, each cry, each voice. So it was that no fear walked with Metaha that night.

Metaha had always found comfort in the night. There was a coolness, a sense of calm. The night was watched over by the spirits of the sky, and Metaha often thought it was in those moments that the spirits could be most easily reached.

As he walked, Metaha heard finally the sound his ears searched for, the great hollow notes of a great horned owl. Its cry pierced the calm of the night, and Metaha stepped briskly. As he walked, Metaha imagined what his return to the village of the Honey Dancers would be like. He painted in his mind the picture of Waseta proudly taking the feather of the owl. He watched his mother's soft hands embrace him.

But there was a battle to be fought, an enemy to be faced, and Metaha had not forgotten the dream. The warning was clear, even if not understood. So it was that the youth walked with great care through the tall trees that were the home of the great horned owls, the creatures who knew the night as a man knows the light of his own fire.

Metaha threaded his way through the trees. Then he heard a great cry. Stepping back, he heard a great bird fly by close to his chest. The bird was too large to be even a horned owl. It was a creature as big as a boy, nearly as large as Metaha.

The youth drew back, a strange feeling coming over him. Then the bird returned, crying out in such a voice Metaha thought the heavens would split. Then the wind stirred in a strange way, and a great feather fell at Metaha's feet.

Metaha picked it up and held it to the moonlight. It was the tail feather of an eagle.

"It is as in the dream," he said quietly. "The eagle has made this gift to me. But it is not the feather of the eagle I was sent to bring."

Metaha took the feather and laid it softly on the ground.

"Thank you, great eagle, but a quest is a thing to be done by a man's own hands. And it is a thing to be done as commanded. I must seek the feather of the owl."

186

Metaha felt the wind blow fiercely. The earth shook, and he trembled for the first time he could remember with the fear a man holds when his life is in danger. It was a bad thing to refuse a gift given by the sky spirits, he told himself. But it was a thing to be done.

Metaha stepped past the feather and on into the darkness. Clouds filled the sky, stealing the moonlight. The youth felt very alone facing the greatest enemy of all, the unknown.

The uneasiness that filled Metaha's heart did not stop his quest, though. On he walked, ever watchful for some sign of the great horned owl. Metaha had never felt anger for any creature, but he knew this owl was his enemy in a way no other creature ever had been: it was only the lack of a feather from this bird that kept Metaha from the warmth and safety of his father's lodge.

Metaha walked on for half the night through the hills of Katai. At last his eyes fell upon a tall hollow tree from which peered two great eyes. His ears picked up the deep, strangely mournful voice of the owl, and Metaha approached the tree.

Metaha's eyes searched for a feather, but owls were creatures of the high places, and no feathers were to be found on the earth. Metaha then looked up at the bird and began his climb to its nest.

In the beginning the owl seemed unconcerned by the presence of the youth. Its great white eyes moved only slightly, watching something else. Then the eyes moved in Metaha's direction, and they froze on the young man as he climbed the tree.

"Great creature of the night air," Metaha spoke

softly as he neared the owl. "I come for the gift of your feather. It is I, Metaha, sent upon the manhood quest that I might prove myself worthy to lead my people. I bear no evil in my heart for you, creature of the night skies."

Metaha had spoken in this way to creatures since the time of the snakes. But the owl seemed not to hear. It was as if the gift Metaha had for speaking to the souls of creatures had been snatched away from him in the time of his greatest need. The owl did not understand. The taking of the feather would be no simple thing.

Metaha reached his hand beside the owl, feeling for a feather. The owl flapped its wings, then clamped down on the youth's hand with its sharp claws. Metaha felt the pain burn through his fingers. He pulled his hand away, looking with wonder at the blood dripping from his fingers.

This is not the way this should be, Metaha thought. This should have been a thing done with ease.

Metaha swallowed his pain and started up the tree again. The owl was still there, angrily crying out in the night. Then it swooped down, flapping its wings against Metaha's face so that he could not see. It pecked at his shoulders with its beak, and Metaha screamed out in pain. Then he lost his grip on the tree and tumbled to the ground.

Metaha was stunned by the fall. He seemed confused. Then it came back to him, the reason for everything he was doing. He reached to his side and took up his bow.

"Creature, are you so mighty that the arrow will not bring your death? Give up your feather that we may

188

both live. Do not blacken my heart with your death!"

But the owl had no ears for Metaha's words. When the youth started up the tree again, the bird swooped down, beating its great wings against Metaha's face and grabbing at the youth's bare shoulders with its claws.

Metaha fought back. He grabbed at the bird, hoping to tear loose a tail feather. The owl moved like the wind, though, and Metaha got only new wounds for his trouble.

Metaha made a last desperate try at the owl, but the creature flew back, then once again forced Metaha from the tree.

"You are a brave enemy," Metaha whispered, trying to regain his wind. "Now you must know the power of my bow arm."

Metaha notched an arrow and looked at the great white eyes peering at him in the darkness. Then he let fly the arrow, and the owl fell lifeless at his feet.

Metaha felt a great sadness as he took from the owl a great tail feather. The creature had been a brave enemy, and it was not courage or strength the bird had lacked. Then the skies became alive with lightning. Blasts of thunder shook the earth, and Metaha grew afraid.

Metaha feared nothing that was of the earth, but what he saw and heard was unearthly. A great sigh crossed the land, and soon torrents of rain beat down on Metaha's shoulders. A chill could be felt, and the youth took up his bow and the feather and began his return to the high place.

"Spirits of the sky," Metaha said as he walked. "You send me a great warning, but I do not see the

189

danger. I have killed the owl and completed my quest. What is there now to fear?"

Still the skies were violent, and Metaha felt the sky spirits shower him with their displeasure. He could not understand how the spirits should be so generous one instant and so harsh the next.

When he climbed back to the high ground, Metaha stripped himself and walked back to the outcropping. The rain washed the blood from his wounds away, and he could feel himself taller and prouder than before. Still, the face of the stars would not shine upon him, and he felt himself cast away from their brightness.

"What has come to be, spirits of the sky?" Metaha asked. "I know I am nothing before you, but you have been my guide. How have I broken my bond to you?"

Suddenly the winds blew in all their fury, and the clouds were swept away. The moon rose high in the sky, and the light of the stars danced upon Metaha's youthful face.

Metaha felt the old warmth he had known from the first time his father had spoken of the spirits of the sky. Again he knew the wonder of their watchful gaze. But there was a sadness on the face of the moon that night, and as morning came, Metaha felt strange. It was as if there could be no brightness in his life. But that could not be. He would soon return to the camp of his father and mother. Soon he would know the softness of others. He would hear warriors sing of his exploits. Little children would reach out to touch the brightness of his hair, hoping they would one day share the greatness Metaha would bring to the Honey Dancers.

Silence filled the air, and the clouds returned.

Metaha made his bed beneath the wall of a cliff. He slept in a dry place that night, full of concern for the future. But his dreams were visited by scenes of great battles, warriors riding to the buffalo hunts, victories over the Comanches. His heart swelled with the greatness he knew must come, and it was only gladness that he knew.

XXII

That next morning broke bright and beautiful. Metaha knew this would be the day he began his homeward journey, and that thought made even the plain rocks and yucca seem beautiful to him. He collected his possessions, then walked to a spring and bathed himself. He bore many scars from his ordeal, but the scars made him look older, more like the warrior that he had become.

He first placed his deerskin breechclout in place, noticing how the mark of the sky that had been burned into his thigh had grown now to be a part of him. He next slipped his arms through the vest, leaving his bare chest proud and strong. Then he wrapped the buffalo hide about his shoulders. It was too warm, though, and he cast it aside. He took the headdress he had made from the buffalo horns and placed it upon his head. Then he cast it, too, aside. Such a headdress was for a great medicine chief, and the people would be angered if a youth returned from the ordeal of manhood wearing such. Instead he placed the wolf's hide over his back, allowing the head to cover his own. In this manner he looked far more like a young warrior.

Metaha placed the other trophies from his quest inside the buffalo hide. When this was done, he stood still, carefully taking out the owl feather. It was this feather that would prove to his people his right to lead the others as chief. Metaha placed the feather under his vest so that it touched his heart.

Last of all he slung his bundle of arrows over his shoulder, took his bow in hand, and began the last of his journey. Metaha knew there were many mountains and great valley between him and the camp of his father, but he walked no longer as a boy who went to the woodlands to prove himself. Now he walked as one who would soon ride the earth as a warrior of the Honey Dancer people.

As he walked, he thought back to the many dangers that had come upon him. He looked at the scars from the owl and the wolf. He glanced at the scalp that hung from his belt, the scalp of the Comanche who had met his death at Metaha's hands. To the spirits of the dead Metaha sang softly an old chant known to his father's fathers.

"Rest gentle in the nights of forever, those I have killed. Be glad to have known the light for even the shortest of times."

Metaha had always thought the chant to be a sad one. Now he knew it told the story of life.

"There is only the light and the darkness, my son," his father had once told him. "We thank the spirits of the sky for the light he sends. We accept the darkness when it comes. Such is the way of things."

"Yes," Metaha said to himself. "There is a way to

things that brings understanding. But much is still not to be understood. The dream. I have seen no eagle's death. This must be yet to come."

Metaha's legs bore him swiftly through the hills of Katai. He journeyed until the time when the sun was no more. Then he began his walk upon the valleys. He wished he still had the Comanche horse, but to wish in such a way is to no purpose.

The sun rose three times to find Metaha in the valley. His moccasins grew thin from the walking. Still on he journeyed, strong with the knowledge that soon he would be home. As he grew nearer, his strides grew more powerful.

Metaha's feet took him swiftly to the great giver of life where he remembered times of swimming as a boy. He tasted the meat of fish for the first time in many days. The last of the dried meat was eaten, and the fruits of the prickly pear soon were tasted as in times of long before.

At last Metaha came close to the village. He did not go to the lodge of his father, but passed through the gate of the ceremonial grounds as the law commanded. There his eyes met with a sight most horrible: A strange head shone in the light beside the gate.

Metaha thought for a moment that the head was some spirit from the past, but then something familiar about it came to him. He walked closer, approaching until he knew what it was. It was the head of Heturu, the boy who, like Metaha, had set out upon his ordeal of manhood. Metaha could see that the hair of Heturu's head had scarcely grown back before his eyes were closed forever upon the world of light. In the clearing beside the gate was what remained of the small boy's body, ravaged by creatures of the night and devoured by birds.

It was a sight that filled Metaha with terror. There was much pain in Metaha's heart. Heturu had never been strong or skilled in the way of a Honey Dancer warrior, and Metaha remembered how Topai had said the ordeal kept the tribe strong by casting aside those too weak to stand their trial. Still Metaha could not help but mourn the loss of one so young at the hands of his own people.

Metaha did not linger beside the hideous head. Instead he walked on, approaching the camp of his people with pride. As he stepped at last into a clearing beside the lodge of his father, Metaha cried out in a loud voice.

"People of the Honey Dancers, I, Metaha, son of Waseta, have returned from my trials. I stand before you having walked the valleys and hills of the world, searching my heart for the strength to be called a man. I have completed my quest, and I stand ready to be taken into the world of men."

There was a great stir among the lodges. Metaha smiled as his mother came close and looked upon his shoulders. His eyes saw the sadness as she looked at the way his arms and legs had grown scarred and hard in the way of a man. Tears fell down her cheeks as she looked at the scalp on his belt, at the fire that burned in his eyes.

Metaha stepped toward her, but Tahoa held out her hand to stop him.

"You are a boy no longer, my son," Tahoa said. "It is to your father that you must come."

Metaha understood. He stood still and watched as

other men and women of the tribe gathered around him. Small children ran over and pinched his skin to see if he was real. Some of them whispered about him, wondering what adventures had come upon him that he should return with the skin of a wolf and the hide of a buffalo among his trophies.

At last Waseta came. The old chief had a frown upon his face. No emotion showed in the man's great eyes, and soon father and son faced each other in silence. Then Waseta smiled.

"All is well," the chief said, clasping the youth in his great hardened hands. "Come to my council fire as a man."

Waseta then lifted Metaha up and held the young man high for all to see. Metaha felt wonderful. His father could never speak words of praise to Metaha before the other people, but the love in the man's hands told the youth all that was to be known.

Tahoa carried the buffalo hide with Metaha's trophies of war, and Waseta carried Metaha. The people followed all of them as Waseta set the youth down in the center of the place of the council fires.

"This night we will sing praises to this youth," Waseta said. "It will be time for feasting. We will eat fresh meat, and there will be dancing. Now it is time for my son to go to the spirit cliffs to speak his words to the spirits of the sky. His journey has been long and hard. Now is the time for rest."

The people shouted and screamed. Then they melted away, going back to their duties in the camp. Waseta slung a great hand around Metaha's shoulder and led the young man away.

"You have done much, my son," Waseta spoke,

pointing to the scalp on the young man's belt. "There will be many stories to sing by the light of our fires. But you must now go to the spirits. Stand naked before them as you have seen me in times past. Remember always that a man is but a man. All that is good comes from the spirits, and it is a man's duty to remind himself of this when he has been blessed with greatness by the spirits."

Metaha nodded to his father, then took the old man's hand.

"Father, I have walked the land alone for many suns. In this time I always remembered the words you spoke to me in my childhood. I have prayed to the spirits many times when great hardships came to me. I have always been answered as I prayed that I might return to make you proud. The spirits smile upon you, my father."

"This they have done from the time they sent you to me, my son," Waseta said, his eyes filled with emotion. "But this moment is for the spirits, not for an old man. Go upon your way."

Metaha turned away from his father and began the climb to the top of the spirit cliffs. When he was at the top of the sacred place, he stripped himself and stood out upon the edge of the cliff, looking to the waters below.

"Great giver of life," Metaha spoke, "grant our people strength and long life. I would have these things before I would have my own life. Give to us the fish to feed us, the waters to bathe and cool us, the shade of your trees, the food from your plants."

Metaha felt the winds stir, and he lifted his eyes to the sky.

"Spirits of the sky, I thank you for all you have brought me," Metaha said. 'I thank you for the victories, for the strength. Now I ask that you grant me the true sight that I might see clearly what is before me. Grant my father a time of contentment in his old age. Grant my mother the love she has always given to all others.

"May I ever be strong enough to endure what is to be. May I always stand tall where I walk, yet be ever mindful that all light comes from the brilliance of your smiles."

Metaha backed away from the edge of the cliff. The wind whispered to him, softly saying that all was well. Metaha was pleased with his words, for he had said the things he felt in his heart, and he had said them in the way of his father. It was now the time for rest. Metaha lay beside a small spring and gave up his thoughts to a gentle sleep.

Metaha was awakened by a gentle hand on his shoulder. He looked up into the face of his father and smiled.

"Are you rested, my son?" Waseta asked.

"Yes," Metaha said, raising himself. "Is there much to be done?"

"You have done all there was to do," Waseta said. "I grieve to see so many scars upon your flesh, but that is the way of a man. Long have I awaited this day, my son, the day when you would sit at my side in the council as a warrior. Now that day has come, and I know that I will come to miss the softness of the child I knew. I will miss the singing that filled my ears and warmed my heart when the hand of winter chilled my bones."

"Yes," Metaha said. "I too will miss many things. I will know no longer the gentle touch of my mother. From this day I must stand upon my own feet, trusting in the wisdom you have given to me as a child."

"Such is the way of life, my son. You must now dress yourself to appear before your people. There you will be honored as a returning warrior is honored. You will relate all that you have done. Then you will be taken to the heart of your people, and there will never be a time when you are a man alone again."

"Yes, Father," Metaha said.

Metaha then dressed himself. He stood proudly before his father. Waseta helped him sling the buffalo hide around his shoulders. Then the two of them walked down the cliff and made their way to the council fire.

Metaha was amazed when he reached the council ring. A great fire leaped skyward, lighting the faces of the warriors gathered all around. The men were dressed in their finest buffalo robes. Many wore the headdresses of eagle feathers made long before. Waseta sat at the top of the circle, and Metaha sat beside the chief. Then Waseta placed the great war bonnet of Katai on his gray head, and the warriors shouted.

"We welcome back the son of the sky, Metaha," Waseta spoke. "He comes back to us after the ordeal of manhood. The great trials are behind him. Now the moment has come for him to tell of his quest."

The people stirred, anxious to hear of Metaha's deeds. Looking around the council ring, Metaha glanced at the smiling faces of his friends. Topai beamed like a star. Even old Boltah was smiling. It had come time for Metaha to speak, though, and he began.

"I set forth upon my ordeal as a boy," Metaha said. "In the days when my flesh was painted with the white dye of boyhood, I roamed the caves and high places of the river . . ."

The people listened intently as Metaha told of his adventures. The warriors smiled as he told of sleeping in the cave amidst the heavy breathing of the wolf. When Metaha spoke of his battle with the deer, Boltah clenched his teeth. The priest grew red in the face when Metaha told of escaping the warriors who came to his camp.

There was a great hush in the council as Metaha related his killing of the Comanche. The people shouted and cried when Metaha passed around the scalp taken from the Comanche.

"It is no small thing to take the scalp of a Comanche warrior in his prime," one of the men said. "For one so young to do so speaks of greatness to come."

The warriors also enjoyed Metaha's story of the buffalo hunt, but they had seen him on the buffalo hunts for many years, and they knew his bow arm had the true aim. Some of them laughed that it had been the buffalo who had come across a great challenge, for it was said that even the wind could not run from the arrows of Metaha.

At last it came to the moment for Metaha to speak of the quest. Many of the warriors looked with harsh eyes at Boltah when Metaha spoke of the trials set before him. When Metaha told of the cliff of eagles, the men stirred again.

"A youth who speaks to the eagles," one of them

said. "Surely this is the spirit of Katai come back to us."

Others heaped praise upon him as he told of the manner in which he had walked across the great waters. When he told of killing the wolf, many wept. Metaha spoke of the pain that had filled his arms and legs, and the people could not restrain themselves. They shouted to the heavens, and Topai and another young man lifted Metaha up for all to see. The warriors crowded around, touching Metaha's arms and slapping his back. Several started singing, and others danced.

The council ring was broken, and Waseta stood.

"We welcome this youth to a world of manhood," Waseta said. "There are those who would bring presents to honor this man."

The warriors drew away from him, and Tahoa came forward. Her face was drawn and he could tell she had been crying. In her hands she carried a beautiful white buffalo robe. He stood still as his father took away the wolf's hide and buffalo cloak, leaving his shoulders covered only by the deerskin vest.

Waseta placed the soft robe around Metaha's shoulders and watched as the brightness of the stars filled the young man's eyes.

"It is a thing of great beauty," Metaha said.

"I will paint it with the story of your ordeal, my son," Tahoa said, withdrawing.

Others than brought forth presents. Topai gave Metaha a beautiful white horse taken from a white man in a raid. Others brought knives, leather pouches, strings of beads, and moccasins. Last of a Waseta took the young man's hand and set his eye pon a new tepee.

"This will be the lodge where you will take your
wife," Waseta said. "To this place you will take your
goods. Here you will spend many winters. Your
children will sing their songs there for you to hear. It
will be a good place, filled with much happiness."

As Metaha felt the warmth of love and praise light
his insides, Boltah stepped forward from the edge of
the circle.

"All this is well," the chief priest said, "but we do
not yet know that this is a man who stands before us.
Boy, do you not have a gift for your people, some sign
that you are the man who would one day lead us to
greatness?"

Metaha realized all had forgotten the feather but
Boltah. Metaha smiled at the man and reached inside
his vest for the feather. As he touched it, his fingers
burned. He had difficulty handling it. Frowning, he
took at last the feather and laid it at the feet of his
father.

Waseta stared at the feather, and the people grew
silent.

"What is this?" Waseta called out, tears filling his
eyes. "What do you bring before your people, my
son?"

"It is the greatest of gifts, Father," Metaha said. "It
is the feather of the great horned owl. I have brought
it from the hills of Katai."

The voices of the warriors cried out in disbelief, but
Waseta silenced them.

"Where did you get this feather?" Waseta demanded.

Metaha looked with great confusion at the face of

his father. The youth did not understand what was happening.

"I sought the feather by climbing a great tree," Metaha said. "I set my hand upon the owl, but it attacked me. Since I could not take the feather in peace, I drew back my bow and put an end to the life of the creature."

The people stirred angrily, and Waseta sat down. Only Boltah smiled. Metaha felt as one naked before the camp of his enemies. He felt a thousand arrows fly into his heart. He did not understand why anger should greet his words.

"What anger is this that fills your eyes, my father?" Metaha asked quietly. "Have I not done what is called for by a man?"

Waseta answered his son only with a silent stare filled with disappointment and anger.

XXIII

Metaha was the only one standing in the council ring who did not understand. It was Boltah who now came forward to say it all.

"There is but one thing to be done!" Boltah shouted. "The spirits of the sky are angry! This one who has brought great courage to many trials would set himself up above the laws of our people. This is a thing that must be dealt with before we are all punished."

"We know the law, Boltah," Topai said, standing up.

"Then let it be obeyed!" Boltah shouted angrily.

"It will be," Waseta said, standing at last. "Tell me, my son, is this a thing done in ignorance?"

Metaha stared into the face of his father. He only now began to understand. Some grave law had been broken, some law that Boltah had never spoken of.

"Have you no words for us, my son?" Waseta asked, his withered old face grown wrinkled and tormented.

"It is as I have always spoken," Boltah said. "No son of the white man can ever be as one of us."

Metaha stared at the hatred in Boltah's eyes. Then Waseta spoke.

"It is the old law from the times before the great ones," the old chief said. "It is said that in the old times, the spirits of the sky looked down upon the Honey Dancers and smiled. As others were turned from men to dust and their souls made to wander the earth, the sky spirits blessed the great warrior chiefs with a second life. The spirits of those bravest of all were taken by the hand of the spirits of the sky and given to stalk the world of the night in the body of the great horned owl. Since the time of the beginning, to touch the creatures of the night sky or to take their lives is to bring the anger of the sky upon the people. Such a thing brings upon the head of the guilty the most painful of deaths."

As the words were spoken, Metaha's heart died. He knew at last that even his worst fears had not equaled the danger.

I have been a great fool, he told himself. I knew the hatred Boltah held for me. I should have spoken to my father of the quest. The spirits warned me, but I could not read their message. The eagle brought me life, but I turned down the gift. A great man as my father would never have set himself above the wisdom of others, would never have turned his eyes from the true light of the sky. I am but a weak man, a man who will never be as strong as my father has been.

"This thing must not be!" Topai shouted, standing before the council. "This cannot be of Metaha's doing. Someone else must be at fault."

"It is the law!" Boltah cried out. "Do we dare risk the anger of the spirits? Do we dare allow this murderer of our fathers to walk free?"

"Silence!" Waseta screamed. "The law allows for justice. Is there something that Metaha would say to us?"

Metaha wanted to explain. He wanted to tell all that he had done. He wanted to shout out his innocence for all to hear. But he knew the others would only laugh at him. It would destroy his father. The fault was Metaha's, and the youth who had faced death at the hands of Comanches and creatures of the night could not fill his heart with fear now. So it was that Metaha said nothing.

"May the law be upheld," Waseta said. "It is to be as it must be."

Waseta waved to four warriors, and they bore Metaha away. Metaha looked back but once at his father. Then the youth let himself be borne away to the spirit cliffs.

The Honey Dancers lived a hard life in a hard land. Such a people had need of hard laws.

Metaha had heard of men punished in many ways, but the law of the owl was one never broken before in his lifetime. He found himself taken to a place on the cliff overlooking the river. There he was stripped of his clothing. Warriors then smeared honey over his body so that all of him was covered but his eyes.

When this was done, the warriors led him to a great bed of ants where he was made to lie down. His wrists and ankles were tied to stakes, and he was left there to lie there under the stars.

As he looked into the heavens, Metaha closed his eyes. A vision of a great eagle crossing the heavens came to him. Then an arrow flew through the air, piercing the eagle's heart. As it fell earthward, Metaha cried inside.

I now know what you meant for me to see, Metaha thought. The eagle had always been symbolic of chiefs. This was the death of a chief, a chief who had never been.

Metaha began to tremble as the ants crawled up his arms and legs. They began collecting the honey. As his fingers twitched, the ants stung him. Now he began to understand the way it would be. The ants would sting his flesh. Then he would die.

Death itself brought no fear to Metaha. It was but a stage between the world of light and the world of darkness. His spirit was one with the earth and the sky, and he knew the sky spirits understood what he was and why he had slain the owl.

But there was the loneliness to be faced, the times of lying upon the cliff as his body grew weak, as the life poured out of him bit by bit.

And there was the other thing, which brought to Metaha the greatest pain of all. That was the disappointment, the betrayal he had read in the eyes of his father. It was the thing that he would have swept away had his hand held the power to do so. But it was not to be, and his heart was sick from it.

As the darkness of night transformed itself into the shadowy light of morning, Metaha heard footsteps on the soft ground above him. They were small feet, and

Metaha strained to see who they belonged to. He moved his head slightly, and his forehead burned with the stings of the ants.

"Do not turn your head, little one," spoke the voice of Tahoa, his mother. "I have only come to pass the hours of your suffering with you that you might not be alone."

Metaha felt ashamed. His mother had not seen him naked since the time of his childhood, and he felt lower than a crawling creature of the river moss.

"Do not look upon me, my mother," Metaha spoke in a whisper. "I am ashamed."

"I know it cannot be your shame that brings you here, little one," she said, her voice broken with sobs. "If you were to speak to your father, then it would be possible to return to the world of the living."

"Did my father say for you to speak these words?" Metaha asked, feeling the ants sting his lips and crawl inside his mouth.

"You know such words will never come from your father," Tahoa said.

Metaha's eyes filled with tears, washing the ants away from his eyelids.

"There is nothing to be said, Mother," Metaha said sadly. "It is a thing decided,"

"Metaha," she said, crying. "I have held you in my arms when you could not yet speak. I have mended the tears in your body and your heart. I have torn my soul in the hours of your absence. Now you have the choice of life and death, and it is death you have chosen. This does not speak of courage."

Metaha looked up into the softness of her face with

great pain in his heart. Her eyes burned with pain.

"I will stay beside you, little one," she said, touching his hand.

"No, Mother," Metaha managed to say. "My pain must be shared only with the stars."

Metaha felt her press his swollen fingers against her own.

"It is only right, little one," she said, still calling him that in spite of the fact he was taller than she was now. "I have always known it was the sky spirit who was your true father."

Metaha wished to speak to Tahoa, tell her what was within his heart, but his lips already burned with the sting of many ants, and pain throbbed through his head. At last he heard her turn and leave him, and the despair of loneliness was once again upon him.

His fingers longed to touch her softness again, but he knew it would only have made his death rest heavier upon her. All that he wished to say was known already in her heart.

As the sun rose high in the summer sky, his body burned from the heat. The rocky ground grew hot as the beds of coals his feet had once walked beside, and his stomach cried out for food.

Metaha's mouth grew dry, and his lips cracked and burned from lack of water. The ants swarmed upon him, stinging his flesh so that it was red and swollen. His throat was burned so that his voice was but a whisper, and his eyes were stung so that he lived now in eternal darkness.

He could still hear, though, and there were those who came to see him. He knew the beginning of each day by the arrival of his old friend Topai. Topai would come and speak to him of many things, of times long ago and adventures they had shared.

"It rests heavy on my heart that it is you who rests in this place, little one with the bright eyes," Topai would say. "You who see always with the true eyes, you who have known the spirits of all creatures, who walk the earth with softness. Yet you will never cry out, and those who hold you near their hearts must keep their tears in silence. Such is the law."

Metaha could feel Topai's powerful hand cast aside the ants from Metaha's face.

"This violates the law, Metaha, but the spirits will not grow angry," Topai said. "It is a thing they would do themselves if they had hands with which to do it. Rest easy, little bright eyes, for the pain you bear is shared by others."

But the saying of that only made Metaha's heart heavier than before.

Metaha's other visitor came amid the greatest howling and dancing he had heard since his return. The visitor came upon smaller feet than Topai, but the stride was firm, and the hand that touched his fingers was strong with the strength of youth.

"How can this be, Metaha, my friend?" asked a voice Metaha recognized as that of Lakadai. "You who rode with the wind, whose bow arm was like the rocks of this cliff. How can it be that you forgot the law of the owl, the most sacred of those told by Boltah? For you who stood tallest among the youths of our people, for you who hold the spirit of Katai in your heart, to suffer so does not speak of justice. They say you have said nothing. Speak now that we might ride together through the summers of our old age, that our sons might ride together to the buffalo hunts."

Metaha felt his heart swell with such words. It was good to know Lakadai at least had survived.

"You have been deceived, Metaha," Lakadai said. "There has never been evil in your heart. I have watched you go to the hunt. I have watched your eyes in the time of your great pain. There is nothing inside you that would lead you to do wrong. It is Boltah. He did not warn you."

Metaha weakly grasped Lakadai's hand. Metaha's voice tried to speak, but the sun had burned away the power of speech.

"I know your heart, my friend," Lakadai said. "You will not show weakness. But there is right in this. I will tell them."

Metaha feebly turned his head, feeling the stings of many ants as he did so. His eyes blinked tears he did not think would come, and Lakadai grabbed his hand firmly.

"Let the strength within me flow into you, my brother," Lakadai said. "Hold onto the life that still burns within you. Do not leave us, old friend. We have need of your spirit."

But Metaha felt the life within him grow weak. His fingers released their hold on Lakadai, and Metaha heard the other youth cry out to the heavens.

"Spirits of the sky, I have climbed to this place to thank you for your deliverance. This I do now. But there is one beside me whose heart is pure as the first

212

snow of winter. Do not turn your face away from him, spirits. Send down your rains to cool his face, your lightning bolts to break his bonds. Grant him life."

But it was not the way of the spirits to strike in such a manner, and Lakadai's voice grew faint.

"I must go, Metaha," Lakadai said. "They gather below to celebrate my manhood. To celebrate when one so pure of heart lies dying is unworthy of our people. I will speak of it."

But the voice of Lakadai carried no weight in the council ring, and the words he spoke were things already known to the people. The law was hard, but the people knew hardness and understood it.

The sun rose and set three times on the face of Metaha. Each time the life in his body lost some of its power. In the darkness of the third night Metaha felt a great numbness fill his toes and fingers. His breathing ceased, and he suddenly saw visions of stars and great winged creatures.

It is the moment of my death, Metaha thought. Let the spirits take me.

For a brief instant his voice returned to him. In a soft voice he cried aloud to the spirits of the sky the old chant known to the Honey Dancers from the time of the ancients.

I journey to the world of darkness,
Knowing I am but a brief song
Carried on the wind.
May my journey be lighted
By the embers of your fires.

As his words died away in the silence of the heavens, Metaha sighed. He wanted to send words to his father, to his mother, to Topai and Lakadai and the others. But his voice was gone now, and he felt the life flow out of him, even as the river flows to the sea. Then his ears heard no longer, and his spirit joined the sky.

The old chief, Waseta, climbed the spirit cliff that very night. It is said that the old man had been able to stay away no longer from the side of the son he loved more than life. But when the old man touched the hand of Metaha, there was no life remaining in the youth.

Waseta cried out to the heavens, tearing his clothes in the old way. A great wailing was heard all that night, and when the man returned, there was no life in his heart.

It is said that when Waseta spoke to the people of Metaha's death, a great cry went up among the old women. Terrible visions came to the medicine chiefs, and many children heard powerful voices in the night. Shadows were said to walk beside the lodges in the twilight, and there were those who feared the sky spirits might strike down the people.

The night of Metaha's death strange fires filled the heavens. A great arrow of flame appeared in the sky, and the moon was eaten one night in the time when it was but young. Great rains poured forth from the skies, and thunder shook the earth. It was a time of great terror, a time full of violence.

As the moon of midsummer was eaten and the last moon of summer was born, the birds and the ants devoured the flesh of Metaha, and his bones were bleached white in the bright sun.

It is said that the place grew to have a power for warriors, and great medicine was to be felt there. As the moons were eaten and new ones born, the bonds loosened, and that which remained of Metaha broke away and fell to the river below. Such was the last of Metaha, who had come to the Honey Dancers as a child, grown strong in the way of his father, and died with the secret of his betrayal locked forever in his heart.

XXIV

In the summers that followed the death of Metaha no greatness came to the Honey Dancers. The snows of winter were deep, and game was scarce. The children cried out in hunger, and the old people walked from the village to seek their deaths in the woodlands beyond. Tahoa, the woman who had echoed the sadness of Waseta's heart, grew thin and died before the final snow had melted. It was said her sadness choked her.

The summer brought new grief. Lakadai, the young man who had shared the trials of manhood with Metaha, fell from his horse as the warriors rode after the buffalo. A great bull ended Lakadai's life as he lay on the ground.

Waseta's hair came to be a ghostly white. Many times the old chief climbed the spirit cliffs to pray to the sky spirits, but his voice lacked power without Metaha at his side. Others say the spirits would have no ears for Waseta's prayers so long as the one who had brought the death of Metaha walked the land.

Only Topai, the strong young warrior who had

befriended the boy Metaha, prospered. Topai led the warriors to the hunt, brought back food in the midst of famine, raided many horses from the white men who now came to the valley of the great giver of life.

Waseta no longer led the young men against the new settlements. His heart was too full of sadness, and he had nothing left for hunting or killing. The whites came, and the tribe grew weaker as the new moons of summer were born.

Three such summers passed, and nothing changed. Few children laughed beside their fathers' fires, and few young men came back from the ordeal of manhood. The Comanches raided from the north, and the white man crept ever closer from the east. There were those who counted the days left to Waseta on the fingers of their hands.

It was near the end of summer when the council gathered to hear Waseta for the final time. The old chief stood before them, speaking in little more than a whisper.

"The time is near when I shall die," Waseta spoke. "There is little power in my heart to stir the spirits. I have not ridden to battle for many moons. It is time for another to take my place."

Boltah was seen to smile, for this was the time the priest had long waited for.

"There is one among us who would lead the people," Boltah said, standing. "My son, Netai, knows the ways of the spirits. His medicine is strong. He will lead the hunt. He will bring honor to our people."

Netai was known to the warriors, and there was a murmur among them.

"How is it that Netai will bring honor to the people when he does not bring honor to himself?" Waseta asked, staring hard at Boltah's face. "This son of yours has fought more battles with the women of our camp than the Comanches. He has brought no meat in the cold of winter. What great medicine is this that would bring hunger into our midst?"

Boltah's face grew red, and he angrily walked away.

"To lead the people," Waseta said, "is a thing that takes a man of strong heart. It demands wisdom and strength. A chief should speak to the spirits, should ride upon the wind, should know the way of honor. His bow must have the true aim, and he should walk the earth with a softness."

The eyes of many were filled with sadness as they heard the words of Waseta. There was not a man among them who was the man the old chief spoke of. Waseta was remembering Metaha.

"He is gone from us," one man said. "We know now some evil fell upon him to make him act as he did. The spirits have punished us for his death."

"He broke the laws," Waseta said, turning away from them. "It was as it must have been. There is one among us who would lead, though. I speak of Topai."

The eyes of Topai filled with surprise, but the other warriors gathered around him.

"Surely Topai is a man to lead the people," they said. "There is honor and greatness among us."

And so it was that Topai became the new leader of the Honey Dancers. There was much dancing and singing among the people as they celebrated the new chief. When Waseta placed the great war bonnet of eagle feathers upon Topai's head, tears flowed freely.

"I wish it was he who stood here," Topai whispered to the old man.

Waseta clasped the young chief's hands, then walked away to be alone with his sorrow.

As Waseta sat alone in the great lodge, Boltah entered. The priest, too, had grown old. The two men faced each other in silence. Then Waseta spoke.

"Leave this place, Boltah," Waseta said. "Leave me to my sorrow."

"Your sorrow?" Boltah asked, his face red with rage. "You mourn a boy you should have killed in his childhood. If you had put him to death as I said, we would be a great people still."

"Leave, Boltah!" Waseta screamed. "He was a good and faithful son. Only in his breaking of the law did he fail, and this he paid for with his life."

"Yes," Boltah said, smiling. "Yes, he paid, but it was not for disobedience. It was for his father's refusal to obey the words of the priest. You have brought my son shame before his people. He will never be held in a high place before the warriors. But I have wounded you in a greater way. I have killed your son as surely as if I had pierced his heart with my arrows."

"You?" Waseta said, laughing. "On your greatest day as a warrior Metaha could have struck you down."

"Ah, but I did not have to put my lance to his throat," Boltah said. "I left the killing to you."

"How so?" Waseta cried out, the tears drying from his hardened face.

"When the others set out upon their quests," Boltah said, "I bid them return with the feather of the eagle. But to that one of the white flesh, I said to return with the feather of the great horned owl. In this way I sealed his fate."

Waseta sat stone-faced for some time. As the old man understood at last the innocence of his son, a great rage burned within his heart. Reaching to his side, Waseta took up an old lance carried in many battles. In a single movement Waseta hurled the lance into the heart of Boltah.

Boltah did not even cry out. There was but a brief sigh. Then the priest fell to the earth in his dying agonies.

Waseta did not pause to look. Instead the old chief ran as a young man runs through his father's fire. He ran through the village toward the spirit cliffs.

"Boltah is dead!" someone cried out.

"It was Boltah who bid Metaha bring back the owl's feather," another said.

The people understood the grief that filled Waseta's heart, and they ran after him to the spirit cliffs. Waseta was an old man, and the others were young. But the spirits gave wings to Waseta's feet, and no one could catch him. When the old man stood at last on the cliff above the place where Metaha's bones had met the waters, he cried out.

"Metaha, my son, I know all," Waseta said. "You whose heart was pure, whose songs brought life to an old man's heart, I come to walk the world of darkness at your side."

It is said the people cried out in protest, but the skies erupted with thunder, and the people stilled their feet. It was then that Waseta cried out the death chant of the Honey Dancers.

* * *

I journey to the world of darkness,
Knowing I am but a brief song
Carried by the wind.
May my journey be lighted
By the embers of your fires.

The wind blew fiercely, ripping open the old man's shirt. He stood there but a moment, closing his eyes a final time. Then he stepped from the cliff and vanished beneath the waters of the river below.

It is said that when the skies grew dark and the stars gazed down upon the earth, a great sorrow filled the spirits of the sky. They grieved that a love so great as that held by this father and son should forever walk the world of darkness.

Since the dead may never walk the world when the sun lights the heavens, the spirits of the sky gave the two, son and father, two shadows of their earthly forms in which their spirits might walk forever in the hours of darkness. From that time the two shadows, the tall and the small, the young and the old, are said to walk beneath the great spirit cliffs.

Nothing remains today of the Honey Dancers, for the whites and Comanches killed the last of their people in a time now long past. The earth has swallowed up their bones, and all they built is now but dust. They were but a brief song carried on the wind.

It is said that love is a thing that bonds men together in a way stronger than wind or time. It is this bond that walks even this day with two shadows beneath a great cliff on the waters of a river now tamed by the hand of the white man. To those whose hearts still burn with the true fires brought by courage and honor, the shadows can be seen and felt and heard to speak softly when the stars are bright and the land is quiet.

What meaning these words have no man today knows. Perhaps the words are a song of battle, a tale of the days of Katai. Perhaps they speak a warning to us all. But the words seem to those who have heard them many times to say, "Do not forget. Remember what once was here."